September Mourning

Charles S. Narasi

September Mourning

Copyright © 2011 by Charles S. Narasi

ISBN 978-0-692-61423-5

C.K.Sampath Iyengar.
(1903-1990)

This novel is dedicated to my dear father who inculcated the value of education, self reliance, service and sacrifice, honesty and integrity in all actions.

IN MEMORY OF MY DEAR FRIEND

DR. ADIRAJ NEMI

(1940-1997)

Left this material world suddenly on September 18th. 1997.

BUFFALO, NEW YORK.

My Special Thanks To:

My dear wife, Karen who is my cheerleader encouraging me to write the novel and helping me immensely with correcting my typing and adding her editing skills .She is a voracious reader of novels of all kinds.

To all my four brothers, Satyanarayan, Ramadas, Bashem and Ananth and my dear sister, Rama who supported me and my family throughout our tough ordeals.

To all our children, Rajni,Kristen,Sujata,Scott and Asha who endured disruption of family unit at a very young age and have grown stronger to face challenges in their lives.

To all my friends from Buffalo and a great community I was privileged to serve for nearly forty years.

Table of Contents

Chapter One

It was a cool September morning in East Amherst, New York. Chandu woke up before the alarm buzzer went on.

"Why do you even bother setting your alarm?" his wife, Kay, would ask.

But being a creature of habit, he did this everyday. His mind was on the procedures he had scheduled at the hospital that morning. He knew he had to face a couple of tough cases, that is technically speaking!

He got out of bed not making too much noise, making sure he would not wake Kay. He could hear her squeaky soft snoring and she was deep asleep, probably dreaming! He looked through the bathroom window out into the backyard. The leaves on the tall trees were beginning to turn color already, signaling an early fall. He looked at the sky and there were some puffy clouds. He tried to use the electric razor but the shaving heads were dull and even had a couple of small holes. He had to buy a new electric shaver! His beard was a challenge to lots of well known razors. The only one that worked well was a German brand. He went back to the old hand razor with shaving gel! That seemed to work fine. Something was on his mind when he was in the shower. He remembered the phone call he got from Raj, the day before, early in the morning.

He got the call at five in the morning. Raj wanted to talk about his work and his kids.

Raj had been a very close friend of Chandu since his medical school days in India. Chandu pulled out of his driveway in his brand new red Volvo, said 'Hi' to the jogging neighbor and headed towards the expressway. The Sun was just coming up brightening the sky adding an orange glow. At that time of the morning the traffic was light and Chandu eased into his lane and drove to the hospital.

He knew that his close buddy, George, would be waiting at the staff room where they would meet everyday and head to the cafeteria. Their usual ritual was to split a toasted bagel and have coffee and juice, discuss the days events. After that, it was off to the endoscopy suite to take care of patients.

Kathy at the reception desk greeted Chandu with a big smile.

"Hi! I hope you are ready this morning! You have six patients for colonoscopy! Marcy will be helping you in room six."

"O.K., Kathy! I am ready, willing and able!!" Chandu said as he changed to the scrubs and headed to room six.

"Good morning Marcy! How are you Richard? Hope you are all cleaned out well for me so that I can take a good look inside your colon!"

"All right, Doc! I hope so too!! I am hungry for a big juicy steak after I get through this today, Doc!"

"Well, you can have it for dinner late tonight, but not for lunch! Right Marcy?"

"That's exactly right! Here comes the good stuff, Richard!" Marcy said as she was injecting the sedative into the intravenous line. Within minutes Richard was in the twilight zone, snoring! Chandu skillfully pushed the long flexible scope through the large intestine and checked for any growths inside. The prep was excellent and he was happy that he was able to do a complete examination in fifteen minutes. Good news for Richard. He does not need this test for another five years. After taking a ten minute break, back to another patient. This one had a non-cancerous polyp detected three years ago and was here for a repeat exam. Again, good news!
No polyps were found.

"What do you say, Marcy! We are moving right along today!"

"You've got four more to go, and I think you are on a roll!!"

Chandu took out a big polyp from another patient and assured him it did not look cancerous although pathology would have to confirm that.

He was down to the last patient and while in the middle of the procedure Kathy came on the intercom and said Chandu had a call from someone.

"Can you please take his number and I will call back right after I am done," Chandu said trying to finish the procedure. He was not expecting any calls and he thought Kay would be at the office to handle any calls from patients. Kay, his wife, had been his office manager and she did pretty much everything, registering the patients to getting them ready for exam and consultation.

He went to his dictation room and finished dictating his procedure report and closed the door to make the call. He felt a little uneasy for some reason but did not think much of it. He dialed the number he was given and his friend, Dr. Prabhakar was on line. His voice was shaky and Chandu knew there was something wrong. "Hey! What's up? Everything O.K.?" Chandu asked.

"I've got some really bad news for you Chandu. I am at Raj's house. Our friend is gone! I mean...I mean he is really gone forever! Please hurry and come over."
Prabhakar was sobbing as he said those words.

Chandu sat back in the chair, closed his eyes for a minute, totally not believing what he heard. How could this be! Raj, a great surgeon who had everything going for him. He had a beautiful home in the rich suburban area where only doctors and lawyers lived. He had been remarried and had three wonderful kids, two boys and a girl, and a very sophisticated wife from India. Chandu quickly finished talking to the patients, told Kathy he might not be in the next day, had some family emergency. Marcy could sense that something was terribly wrong but did not want to push for answers from Chandu.
"Take it easy, Chandu! Take care of yourself!"

Chandu hurried to the parking lot and started the car, heading to Orchard Place. He could not come up with any answers no matter how hard he tried.

Why would Raj die suddenly when he had such a great life. Chandu knew that Raj had minor health problems, early diabetes which was well under control. Only two weeks ago he had a bout of flu.

He arrived at Raj's driveway where an emergency vehicle was parked. There were several people around, and Prabhakar rushed to meet and hug Chandu.

"Raj hung himself in the basement this morning," he continued, "I got a call from Malathi , his wife. She went looking for him early this morning and was shocked when she went to the basement. Raj had hung himself and was dangling like a rag doll!!"

Chandu felt like he was stuck by a dagger and stood still for a second. he couldn't fight back the tears running down his cheeks. As he was staring at the sky, the emergency crew lifted the body to the ambulance.

"Please don't take him! I must see him! I must see my friend," Chandu cried.

"Yes, Doc, you can see him! But we have to take the body to the morgue at the hospital. Make it quick!"

Chandu could only see the black and blue marks on Raj's neck and a swollen face. He gently touched his face and kissed him goodbye and said,

"May your soul rest in peace. I will miss you, my friend, for now but we'll meet again in heaven someday!"

The ambulance sped away and Chandu looked at Malathi and said, "Oh! My God!" and he gave her a quick hug and took her into the house.

"Do you want one of us to bring the kids home, Malathi?" Chandu asked.

"I really don't want to face them, what I am I going to tell them? Your daddy is gone for ever? Especially Reena, my daughter! She was so close to her daddy. What do I do? Oh! God! Why me? why me?" she cried.

Prabhakar said he would get the kids and prepare them for the worst news. She nodded and he left quickly to bring the kids home.

Chandu looked at Malathi and asked her if he could go down the basement and take a look. He did not wait for an answer from her and went down the stairs. As he got down and saw what was left of ropes hanging from the ceiling of the basement, a shiver went through his body. How was this possible for a young man to do this, this precise with no help! Again there were no easy answers. He stood in silence for a couple of minutes and muttered prayers softly.

Tears were running down his cheeks and a friend was no more! Thirty five years since the time they graduated from medical school, how things had changed in a split second! He came back up and saw Malathi in a fetal position laying on the couch, sobbing. He sat beside her, held her hand and said,

"Malathi, we have to think about Raj's funeral arrangement and notifying all the relatives about this tragic news. Do you have any idea? We have to contact a funeral home and, of course, there will be cremation. I am sorry I have to bring this all up, but we have no choice!"

Malathi nodded and wanted to wait for the kids to come home with Prabhakar. Reena and Jitu ran in screaming and crying and Malathi hugged them both as tight as she could and let them cry their eyes out.

Prabhakar made some phone calls to get in touch with the funeral home in Orchard Place not too far from home. Later that afternoon, the hospital would release the body to the funeral home for preparation. The preliminary report from the coroner confirmed cause of death as asphyxiation due to strangulation. There were no signs of heart disease or any complications related to his diabetes. Chandu made phone calls to other mutual friends and also realized he had not talked to Kay who was still at the office.

"Kay! We have to cancel our office hours for today and tomorrow. My buddy, Raj, suddenly died this morning and we have to make all the arrangements for his funeral. I will be home late and I will fill you in all the details. O.K., honey?

Don't worry about me! I will be all right and I love you!" Chandu hung up the phone. He did not want to tell Kay on the phone how Raj had died.

Buffalo News was contacted and the obituary would appear in the paper the next day. After a long dreadful day he was ready to go home.

Chapter Two

The year was 1962 and Chandu along with his friends were waiting to hear about the results of their final examination to graduate from medical school. He called Raj and asked him to join the group at a restaurant across from the medical school. This was the same place they would go for lunch between classes. The place was small but clean and served good food. The waiters always took good care of the future doctors. Chandu's favorite snack was masala dosa with hot chutney, the hotter, the better. A strong cup of coffee followed. This time they would eat a whole dosa. Usually they would split the dish and also have half a cup of coffee each and split the bill. But this time, it was special. Culmination of years of hard work. Very soon they would start working in the hospital and receive a stipend. Raj came in a little late but joined the rest of the guys. Conversation revolved around what everyone would do after the internship which would last twelve months in various specialties of medicine. Most of the guys would stay in Bangalore and maybe start a private practice.

They were almost done with their lunch and asked for the check from the waiter. They all chipped in their coins and Chandu was in charge of collection. When they were about ready to leave Prabhakar came running and said, "The results are in, results are in. Come, they are posted on the bulletin board at the medical school". They were all anxious, and with their hearts pounding they hurried to the medical school to get a glimpse of the bulletin board. Chandu, Raj and Pabhakar made it through. Some of the others were not so lucky. They had to retake the exam.

Chandu and Raj high- fived and let out a loud scream. They called their parents and let them know the results.

Raj said "All that combined study we did and taking parts of the cadaver, like the brain and liver, home to study really helped, right Chandu?"

Chandu laughed and patted Raj's back and said "Let's celebrate this evening with a beer and mutton biriyani".

"You know, we are not supposed to eat meat or drink beer!", Raj said.

Chandu replied, "You know, my father says, you are a doctor and you can do what you want!".

"So, you have his blessing?"

"Well, sort of. So long as we are careful".

"O.K. I will see you at Mustafa's near the city market at 6:00 p.m."

They had to catch the city bus to get to their respective destinations.

Chandu's father was waiting at home and he was all smiles and had that proud father look on his face.

"You did what I was not able to do," he said. Chandu remembered the times his father would tell him how much he wanted to be a doctor, but his father could not afford to send him to medical school. Chandu's father worked for the government during the days of British rule and retired when he was 45 years of age and was collecting pension. Chandu was very fortunate to enter medical school on merits, good grades in pre-med courses.

He thought of the interview he had with the professors and dean of medical school. One professor was well known for his writing skills. He was a humorist and had published several books. Chandu's resume included his acting and writing skills. The professor was very impressed with these and Chandu thought that might help him. That did help him, along with his grades, to secure a seat in medical school.

Raj was prompt to show up at Mustafa's restaurant and his brother had gotten a loaner from a car dealer friend of his. He was the designated driver. They sat down at the dinner table and ordered a couple bottles of King Fisher lager beer. The waiter brought the beer with tall glasses and a few munchies that included hot nuts and pappadam, favorite snacks of south India.

"Cheers! May all our dreams come true." Chandu said, clinking the glasses. "Cheers!" they all echoed and started sipping the cold beer.

"I can't wait to start our work at the hospital. I am so excited that you and I are going to be in the same unit for two months, Raj."

"Yes, I think that is great, especially to be on call on the same nights."

"The best thing is, we are going to be assisting in surgery and we have a great professor to teach us."

"What do you think we will be doing after the twelve months of internship? You have any clues, Raj?" Chandu asked.

"Well, remember what we have been talking about for the last two years? It's America, baby, U S of A!!"

"I know, when we saw the movie 'Niagara', with Marilyn Monroe, that's where I want to be!! Right Raj?" The effect of the beer was taking hold slowly!

The waiter brought the biriyani dish and they were busy eating now. This Pakistani restaurant made the best mutton biriyani, hot and spicy. It went very well with the beer. When they finished, Raj's brother was ready to take them home.

Their internship was to start the following Monday at Victoria Hospital. They were both assigned to the surgical unit, ward number eight, which had a hundred beds. There were patients who had surgery and those waiting for surgery as well. They would work from eight in the morning `til nine at night, and take night calls every third day. The schedule was tough. Assist the surgeon in the morning and make rounds in the evening. This included preparing patients for next day surgery and taking care of operated ones. The days were very exhausting and they hardly had time for a quick snack between cases.

Chapter Three

Raj had dressed well this night, splashed on an expensive aftershave lotion just before he went to the eighth ward. As soon as he waked in, his eyes were wandering around looking for Gina. The older nurse was at the desk and Gina was in the dispensing room preparing the drugs. It was around 10 p.m. and the coffee room was next to it. Raj went to get a cup of coffee and stuck his neck out to get a glimpse of Gina's face. Gina knew she was dealing with two new interns and she was contemplating to do something funny on their first night call day. She came out of the room and looked at Raj and said, "Dr. Raj, can you take this bedpan to number six. He had the call button on. Please hurry!" Raj blindly obliged, only to find out later that was not his job!! The nursing attendant was responsible for this! Gina started laughing aloud, came over to Raj and touched his shoulder and said, "I am sorry, doctor, I was just joking." Raj felt a strange sensation and he was still feeling Gina's touch. That was an ice breaker and they both laughed.

Chandu could hardly control his laughter while he watched all of this.

"Hey, you are not going to tell the other interns about this, right?" Raj asked.

"You mean the bedpan thing or you hitting on Gina!!" Chandu replied. "Don't worry about it, it stays with me, Raj!"

Next day during the morning conference with the attendings, all the interns were teasing Raj about the bedpan!! So much for the secret! Days went fast while the two continued to work in various services, the tetanus ward where there was total darkness, the injection room where they took care of hundreds in long line waiting for shots, typhoid, cholera, T.B., etc., etc. Men and women, young and old stood for long hours waiting their turn.

The maternity ward rotation was very tough on the guys. Three or four women were Delivering babies at the same time!

Some nights they would not close their eyes for even fifteen minutes. But they knew how much better their training was and they would be ready to face the future.

"So, are you going to ask her out, Gina, are you, Raj? Chandu asked. "Well, I am thinking about it. What if she says No?', Raj replied.

"Only way you find out, you have to be bold and ask her. All she can say is 'Yes or No,' right?"

"I know she likes me by the way she tries to assist me when I am taking care of a patient. She leans over so close to me that I can almost feel her face. I can smell her perfume!!" Raj sounded excited.

"Then why don't you ask her today? I think she's off tomorrow and we have half a day off. Maybe you can take her to a movie!" Chandu suggested.

"O.K. I will ask her when I get a chance," Raj whispered.

Chandu pulled Gina aside and told her Raj needed her near bed eight where he was Changing dressing on a wound. Then he winked with a smile and walked away.

Raj saw Gina coming to him and his heart started pounding. He was now thinking about what to say next. It is not customary in Hindu faith to ask a girl for a date. What would the parents think? Even in medical school this was a no, no!! About one third of the class was ladies but they all sat on one side of the class room!! Though they were allowed to work together on cadavers in anatomy class, they were still not approachable in social settings! The guys made the best of it during dissections, trying to be as close to the ladies as possible!

"I want to ask you something, Gina! You have a day off tomorrow, right? What are you doing in the afternoon? Maybe we can go to see a movie. There is a good Hitchcock movie in Contonment: There is also a very good restaurant nearby and we can have dinner after the movie. What do you think?" Raj waited for an answer.

"You know, Raj. I really like you. I think you are a great doctor and I am glad to be working with you here. If the attendings come to find about this, I mean us going out, that may be bad for you! Let's think about this for a while and if we do go out, it has to be done very discreetly. O.K.?" Gina stroked his face gently and walked to her desk.

When Raj walked in the next morning, Chandu could see that Raj's face had a triumphant glow and he felt that Gina had accepted Raj's offer.

"What happens next? You think you are going to pursue this relationship seriously, do you Raj?" Chandu asked.

"First things first, Chandu. I am not jumping the gun. See what develops!"

"We have to think of our parents and their wishes, you know. Never forget that," Chandu was emphatic.

"I know, I know. I am not going to be irrational about this, man," Raj said. They got busy the rest of the day with surgery and taking care of new patients. Three days later they were having lunch at the hospital cafeteria and Raj sat silent for a while. This was rather unusual for him.

"Is everything O.K.? You haven't said a word since we sat down," Chandu enquired.

"Well, I did go out with Gina yesterday. We went to the movie and I took her out to the Blitz restaurant for dinner We listened to some new disco music. I thought she was having a good time. She wouldn't drink any alcohol, and I had one beer. We just talked a little bit about our families. I didn't learn much about her. You know what? There wasn't any spark!!" Raj finished.

"So, you're not going to ask her out again are you?" Chandu smiled.

"I guess not! You know that nursing assistant, Latha? What do you think of her? I would like to put my arms around her if I can!" Raj asked.

"You know, I think you have too much androgen in your system, boy! You better cool it before we get into trouble with the nursing director!" Chandu shook his shoulders.

"I guess you are right. But when we go to the states, USA, I mean, we can do whatever we want. We will be away from the family, agree?"

"Well, that's totally different. First we have to pass the qualifying exam. By the way, the exam is in Madras and is only two weeks away. Are you well prepared?" Chandu reminded Raj.

"Yup, you know that US library by the city hall has everything we need. They have exam preparation review material that we can borrow and study at home. Why don't we go there this weekend?"

"Sure, we can do this. We have to pass this exam. That's our goal." For the time being they tried to put away thoughts about girls.

Chapter Four

The express train to Madras was speeding down the tracks. People were hanging on the railings every which way. The train was full. They had a first class cabin reserved and were traveling comfortably. It was also a dining car and had very good lunch and hot beverages. They looked out the window and the green fields of rice paddy spread for miles and miles. Raj was dosing off and Chandu was thinking about the exam. They were to arrive in Madras at 6:00 a.m. and they had to be at the medical school by 10:00 a.m. They took a taxi from the station and were on time to arrive at the school.

On the way, they noticed streets with strewn garbage, animal waste along with wandering cows and buffaloes. The railway station was located in a poor neighborhood of the town. Thatched huts with little children, some with little or no clothing standing by and waving to the people in the taxi created a striking scene.

There were about a hundred candidates that were taking this qualifying exam called E.C.F.M.G. (Educational council for foreign medical graduates). Passing this exam would open doors to various medical institutions in America.

Chandu and Raj thought they had done their best and were hoping they would ace this exam. Only, they would have to wait six weeks before they could plan for the future. However, they were confident.

After they finished with the exam, they were walking down the street. By the sidewalk they saw an older man with shaggy hair and bearded face sitting with a sign showing a large palm. "Know your future. Get a palm reading. Only five rupees," the sign read.

"Hey, Raj, I want to find out how good this guy is. Shall we ask?" Chandu asked with curiosity. "Sure, why not, let's," Raj agreed.

The old man took the money first and read Chandu's palm. He had to see both palms. The left hand reveals what is inherited and the right, what is acquired!

"You are going to travel very far and you are going to make money," the old man said. "You will be separated from the family for a very long time. But I only see good things coming your way!" he said. Then he turned his attention to Raj and took his hand.

"You are also going to be doing a lot of travel and earn lots of money," he said. He kept his eye on the life line of the right palm of Raj and looked up at the sky for a second. That was the end of the session. He did say that both of them would have a nice life and would be blessed with kids.

They headed back to the railway station to catch the night train back to Bangalore. They both were excited about the prospects of going abroad, especially to the United States. Some of their classmates were going to England to pursue higher training and education. Chandu and Raj were not fascinated with England at all, maybe because of the history! After gaining independence from the British, they were not willing to go there and be treated like second class citizens! Also, they knew the training in the U.S. was hands on, unlike the British system.

They had to start looking for hospitals in the U.S. where they would start internship. Since they already had a great exposure to various medical situations, they would have an upper hand.

The last three months of their rotation went fast, and at six weeks they received a congratulatory letter notifying them of getting passing grades in the E.C.F.M.G. exam. They were ecstatic about this, and maybe the old man's predications would come true. Great palm reading, they thought. Both Chandu and Raj started doing some research into U.S. hospitals, and they were particularly anxious to see if they could start the training early. Usually training internship started in July at most of the teaching hospitals.

They had received applications from Albany, New York; Detroit, Michigan; and Buffalo, New York.

Buffalo, New York had immediate openings for two interns because of unexpected departure of two of their interns. The brochure they received was very impressive, had a great colorful picture of Niagara Falls!!

When they saw this, they were thinking of the movie, 'Niagara,' and the gorgeous Marilyn Monroe!!

"What do you think, Raj? Looks like we got our wishes! Within two weeks we can be there and start our internship in March! Wow!!" Chandu shouted. Raj was equally excited, as well.

"Now I think we have to convince our parents. Your mother, especially, Raj.." Chandu knew Gouramma, Raj's mother, was quite hesitant about sending her son so far away!

"You will have to persuade my mother, Chandu. Only you can do it as my closest friend! Will you talk to her? Why don't you come for breakfast tomorrow and we can talk about this. O.K?" Raj begged.

"All right. I will be there. See you tomorrow. I know your mother is a great cook and I will come hungry." Chandu headed back home. As for his parents, his father was always encouraging all the children to pursue whatever it was in the line of education. "Nobody can steal your knowledge and you will go far in life. Just be yourself and don't go after money. The money will follow you if you do good in whatever you do." That was the best advice he had drilled into all of his six children. Chandu was the middle child of the family, but was never treated as one!

Gouramma was waiting for Chandu's arrival. She greeted him with a big smile and asked, "Hope you are hungry, Chandu? Have your breakfast first, and then we will talk." She started serving the great dishes she had prepared, sweet cereal called Kesari Bath with fine saffron threads and cashew nuts full of flavor, also chickpea fritters called Masala Vadai with mint leaves, good and spicy. She also prepared a drink made with almond paste, brown sugar and heavy cream. Chandu could not resist asking for seconds! After the last sip of the drink, Gouramma sat next to Chandu and held his hand. With a choking voice she asked Chandu, "Will you promise me that you two will stay together always and keep a close watch on Raj that nothing bad happens to him?"

Chandu replied, "You know he is my fifth brother as far as I am concerned. Please don't worry about us. We will look after one another and with all of your blessings and God's, we will be safe!"

"I trust you, Chandu. You are like a son to me. You will have all of our good wishes and blessings." Tears were running down her checks as she held both of their hands tight, not willing to let go.

They had to travel back to Madras for their Visas. Also they had planned to visit the famous Tirupathi temple and see the Almighty God at the Seven Hills. This was a must before they would embark on their overseas adventure. No one in either family had been abroad. This is why this was so special. There were tens of thousands of devotees lined up to see God Venkateswara when they got up the hill by bus and arrived at 5:00 a.m. By the time they were able to see the deity, it was almost 9:00 a.m. But they were very happy about the visit and knew all would be well, and they would make it to the U.S.A.

Both families had arranged for a charter bus to the airport. Lots of family members and friends wanted to see them off and say, "Bon Voyage!"

Chandu and Raj were treated like royalties, decorated with garlands made with jasmine and roses. Lots of advice to both!

"Be very careful, watch for black people! American girls can lure you! Don't give in to temptations, alcohol, drugs! We know you guys will be O.K." Then tears and hugs, and finally they got on board the plane. It would be a very long time before the families would see them again.

Chapter Five

This was a massive jumbo jet 747, Lufthansa, a German airline with a great reputation for comfort and service. After the plane reached the desired altitude, stewardesses came around offering free drinks and snacks. They both ordered scotch and club soda, their favorite dink, other than beer. A package of roasted peanuts were given as well. They both held their drinks and said, "Cheers. This is for us!!" They sipped the good tasting scotch slowly and enjoyed the snacks. Later that night there was a nice movie they could watch. They had the head sets on and started listening to the music. Raj closed his eyes and before long he was snoring. Chandu tried to stay awake to watch a second movie but the day's events caught up with him and finally he closed his eyes. Next thing they knew, the flight attendant was waking them up to serve breakfast. Frankfort and London were the next two stops and they would arrive in New York, JFK airport at around 8:00 a.m., local time. A very long journey. Almost 31 hours since they boarded the plane in Bangalore! As the plane started it's descent to JFK, their excitement grew in leaps and bounds!

The pilot pointed out the landmarks, the Statue of Liberty standing tall! This was the sight they would never forget. All those tall sky scrapers looked enormous. This is what they had expected to see and experience.

The plane finally landed, and soon they would get to the baggage claim area. The airport was huge and filled with people from all around the world. So many different languages and sounds.

After they gathered their luggage, they went through customs and were approaching 'transportation.' They were supposed to catch a shuttle to LaGuardia airport to reach their final destination, Buffalo, New York. That would be a forty minute flight.

They did not know there was free transportation, a shuttle service to the other airport.

They hailed a taxi cab and reached LaGuardia airport. The cab fare came to sixteen dollars. Chandu looked at Raj and said, "I have only eight dollars. You have eight also. I guess that will take care of the fare." When they left India, the Reserve Bank would only allow them to carry eight dollars each!! Now after they paid the cab driver, they were penniless for sure! "Welcome to America!" they thought!!

The plane landed in Buffalo around 2:00 p.m. Fortunately for them, there was a senior resident of medicine awaiting their arrival! He was sent by the hospital medical director.

"Thank God you are here. We don't have any money left! We were worried how we would get to the hospital," said Chandu, relieved.

They were sitting in a nice red Buick and were only twenty minutes from the hospital.

Both had a nice room to share up on the sixth floor of the hospital. After a very long and tiresome day, they were ready for bed. They were instructed to meet with the medical director the next morning along with other medical interns and residents. They got up early in the morning, put their long white coat on, and went down to the cafeteria. They had a special doctors' section. Bacon, sausage, pancakes, scrambled eggs, home fries, juice and coffee were on the menu. Only fries and pancakes appealed to them. They needed a lot of hot sauce to add flavor!!

After the breakfast they met with the medical director, Dr. Whepple, a big man, with a bald head and thick glasses. He greeted the new interns with warmth and handshakes.

"I expect the very best from all of you," he said with a strong, commanding voice. "We are here to help you, me and the other attendings. Don't think the nurses know 'nothing.' They know more than you. You can ask for their help. O.K.? Any questions?" Everyone nodded no.

"Oh, by the way. I want to see you two, Chandu and Raj! Follow me to my office," he said.

When they got to his office, the secretary, Geraldine, gave them a hundred dollars each, in cash, and said, "This is your advance payment for one week. We found out that you had no spending money!"

The feel of real money made them shake inside!

"Wow! That's like six thousand rupees!! I can't believe this." Raj said.

"This is great. We can buy some warm clothes now. You know they are predicting snow today! We have never seen it except in the movies!" Chandu said in excitement.

They were assigned to the Emergency Room duties. Since they already had worked in surgery in India, this would be easier for them. Few trauma cases, few people with chest pain turned out not to be heart attacks. They saw a few patients with stroke, paralyzed on one side. They had to take care of some lacerations with sutures, etc. The nurses were very impressed by the young interns' skills.

It was time for lunch and when they came to the cafeteria, the smell of lamb chops was pervading the air. That did not appeal to them. After they looked at the various items on the menu, they were not sure what to try! Roast beef that looked like shoe leather and raw spinach and greens fit for a goat! They lost their appetites. One of the senior medical residents who was from India suggested a slice of pizza. He said, "Sprinkle these hot pepper flakes and it will taste good." Raj and Chandu took that advice and tried a small portion. "Not bad. I think we can eat this. At least we can't go hungry! We will eat this every day," Chandu said.

It was a lot of adjustment to try and like things they would eat. Of course there was the kitchen on the sixth floor, where they would taste bread and put jam or jelly and enjoy it. It took them months before trying a hot dog. They were afraid to eat dog meat! It took a lot of convincing that the meat was not from dogs!

Days and weeks were passing by fast. They had their first exposure to snow. Like little kids, they would play in the snow, throwing snow balls at each other. Some evenings they would bundle up and walk in the snow, up and down the side street, only to come back nearly frozen. Up on the sixth floor they had a game room with table tennis and a poker table There was a big television to watch the shows.

The other interns in their group and the senior residents were very friendly. One of them, O'Hurley, an Irish medical resident, was very playful.

Next door to the hospital was the nursing students' dormitory, and O'Hurley would invite a few girls to join the interns for dinner at Chin's, a very popular Chinese restaurant in downtown Buffalo. Ten or twelve of them would all meet at the restaurant, drink beer, eat nice spicy Chinese food, listening to the juke box music. The girls were loud and giggled a lot, while the boys were trying to impress them. Mostly the boys picked up the tab, with an occasional offer from the girls!

That night was a free from call night, and they both were relaxing up on the sixth floor lounge. The Ed Sullivan show had been advertising the Beatles, the new singing sensation group from U.K. This would be their debut appearance in America. The show was exciting and the unique nature of their songs and lyrics were very impressive. Screaming young girls in the audience and the overall response was overwhelming, to say the least. The Beatles were here to stay, they thought!

At 11:30 p.m. was the 'Tonight Show' with Johnny Carson. He was their favorite comedian! They enjoyed 'Karnak, the Magnificient,' the most.

Chandu turned to Raj and asked him, "Hey, I see you spend a lot of time going to the radiology department. Is there something I should know?" and smiled.

"Well, you know Lizzy, the x-ray tech, that pretty blonde? Wow! I would like to ask her out! What do you think?" Raj asked.

"You know she has a steady boyfriend. That guy, Eddy, who also works there. You think you will have a chance?"

"I am a doctor and he is only a tech! Who do you think she would prefer? I certainly think she would pick me!! Besides, I am more handsome!" Raj was very proud of his looks!

"All the best to you. Go ahead and ask her out," Chandu encouraged. Chandu remembered that they were supposed to look at an apartment this weekend. The place was very close to the hospital, and they wanted to move out of the sixth floor and have their own place with separate rooms and a nice kitchen! Chandu always loved to cook and a nice, big kitchen would be ideal! He had been a cook when the brothers shared an apartment during their college days. One brother was a helper, chopping the veggies, etc., and the older brother was a good cleaner! Raj had no experience in cooking since his mother, Gouramma, never allowed him in the kitchen! They looked at the apartment on Ashland Avenue. It was a two story building and three bedrooms were upstairs. The owner had kept the place in good shape. The place was furnished, as well. The rent was reasonable since the two would split the expenses. They decided to sign a two year lease. They would have their own place to study and also to entertain!! They were anxious to have a party at this new place.

"It would be great if we can invite the guys and have them bring over girls. I can do all the cooking," Chandu volunteered.

"I will talk to O'Hurley. He is a great organizer. We have to do some shopping. There is a Indian grocery store near the Vet's Hospital on Bailey Avenue. Let's go this evening. 0.K?" Raj had his plans.

"Remember, we need lots of snacks and beer by the case." Chandu suggested. "The guys will bring some, too. There should be enough. We have a record player and we will have fun! Are you going to invite Lizzy?" Chandu asked.

"Yes, how about you? That girl, Vicky, on 3-North, she really likes you!"

"I think she will go out with anybody! Maybe she will do, this time," Chandu said, winking at Raj. "We have to clean the rug and the bathroom. After all, this is our first celebration in the new apartment."

They went to the Indian grocery store and bought the various spices for the chicken curry that Chandu was going to cook. They got back to the apartment and Raj volunteered to clean the place. Chandu was the master chef in charge of the cooking! He liked to be the king in the kitchen and liked to work alone. Cooking came very natural to him. He started chopping the onion, garlic, ginger and little chili peppers. They both liked very spicy foods. They were not so sure about the girls. O'Hurley liked spicy taste as well. Chandu decided he would prepare the dish medium hot and if someone wanted, they could add more chili peppers. The aroma of various spices filled the air and was sure to bring on everyone's appetite.

By 5:00 p.m. girls and guys started coming. Raj had done a great job with cleaning the front porch, living room and bathroom!

The guys had brought with them more beer, chips and dip and other snacks. A couple of girls brought a cake and cookies. The stereo was playing pop music! They got into the beer and snacks.

The place got filled with the crowd, and the music got louder. Everyone was having a good time dancing and singing! Lizzy was there without her boyfriend, and Raj was ecstatic! Vicky showed up as expected. She had a crush on Chandu, but the feeling was not mutual! That didn't stop Vicky from grabbing Chandu and asking him to dance with her. He did it just to be nice to her. He never realized that she would be hounding him almost every day after the party, expressing interest in being his girlfriend. Chandu stopped taking her phone calls and tried to disguise his voice, pretending to be someone else! Only after Vicky found out that Chandu had his eye on another junior Irish nurse on the fourth floor the calls stopped. Her name was Michelle, a petite blonde with blue eyes and a million dollar smile. Her eyes would sparkle whenever she worked with Chandu. After much effort he found out that her boyfriend was sent to Vietnam about a year ago. But she had a very special attraction toward Chandu.

He was on night call that night and Michelle was the night nurse. He was making the midnight rounds and spotted her. She greeted him with a big smile.

"I see you are on call tonight. I wanted to tell you that all the attendings like you very much. They don't want to be bothered if you are on call! They really trust you, and so do the patients that you take care of!" she continued. "How do you like your new apartment? I heard you guys had a nice party last weekend. How come I wasn't invited?" she winked. Chandu blushed slightly and said, "You can come to the next one! As a matter of fact, why don't we go on a double date. My buddy, Raj, will bring someone. You like Chinese food don't you? We can go to Chins on Main Street."

"That would be nice," she said and squeezed Chandu's fingers gently! Chandu was on top of the world! Could this be really happening? He had to pinch himself to make sure this was not a dream!

"How about that boyfriend in Vietnam?" Chandu was not going to worry about him for now.

The rest of the night was uneventful, for a change, except for a cardiac patient that needed an EKG. He had no problem doing that while Michelle watched him with admiration!

Raj had made up his mind that Lizzy was out of reach for him and started looking for a new girlfriend to date.

There was this tall, thin, very pretty redheaded nursing assistant working in surgery. Raj was exceptional with his skills in surgery and that was what he wanted to specialize in. Lynette was a young lady, probably in her late teen years, very attractive. She had an idea that Raj was paying unusual attention to her and trying to be close to her whenever he would. She liked his looks and his surgery skills. When the senior surgeons would praise him, somehow she felt shivers run through her body. She was attracted to him, just as much, and she was waiting for the opportunity to go out with him.

When Chandu mentioned about the double date, Raj thought about Lynette and approached her in the scrub room the next morning.

"Hey, Lynette. My buddy, Chandu, will be taking Michelle, the nurse on the fourth floor, out to dinner at Chins. How would you like to join me, so all four of us can have fun. What do you say?"

Lynette nodded and said, "I have a day off tomorrow also. That will be great. Only thing is, my mother wants me back home by 11:00 p.m."

"No problem. We can do this," Raj assured her.

Chandu and Raj were thrilled at the prospect of going on this special double date! Chandu had recently bought a green Ford Falcon, an old, well maintained car. He was the first one to pass the driver's road test and get a license. He washed and polished the car, cleaned the inside and wanted to impress the girls. They picked up the girls from their homes and drove to Chins. They ordered a pu-pu platter, enjoyed a fancy pineapple drink with a colorful umbrella, kung pow chicken with peanuts and stir fried vegetable rice. After the dinner, they were given four fortune cookies. Michelle's read, "Enjoy present company!" Lynette's read, "Great things come soon." Chandu's read, "Good fortune follows dream." Raj's . . . "Keep eyes open for fruit in front." They all laughed!

During the dinner, the juke box was playing great number one hits on the pop chart. They got back into the car, and on the way home, Raj and Lynette were enjoying nice conversation. They held hands and Chandu could see them hug and kiss. Michelle held Chandu's hand and let him pay attention to the traffic. When Michelle got dropped off, Chandu walked her to the door and held her in his arms. Their eyes met, and he could see the sparkle in her eyes. He bent down and gently kissed her soft lips and held her tight for a few minutes.

"I had a great time, Michelle, and I can't wait to do this again," Chandu said, waving goodnight to her. She disappeared through the door and he started back home. That night, both Raj and Chandu were very happy with how things turned out that day.

Chapter Six

Dr. Barone, an Italian doctor, owned a couple of race horses which ran in Hamburg harness racing track. The track was only about twenty minutes drive from the hospital. Chandu and Raj both worked with him in surgery assisting in operations. He had been asking the boys to come to the race track when his horses were running. Apparently he had a very good jockey, Vince Aquino, who had won several races. That Friday, his one horse, `Beat the Drum' was running in the eighth race. Dr. Barone said, "You guys can bet on this horse. You will definitely make money."

They went to the race track, a very crowded place, full of excitement. Hundreds were lined up in the front watching the horses trying out before the race. This was a totally new experience, and after they got a program book, started looking at the previous winners and losers! Dr. Barone met them and bought them beer and pretzels. He showed them how to bet and what the odds mean. All those different words to learn . . . the daily double, exacta, trifacta, etc.! They did learn fast. The eighth race came and Dr. Barone's horse, 'Beat the Drum" was in third post position. During the trial run, the horse looked very good. Both Raj and Chandu bet ten dollars to win and picked an exacta of 3 and 7. The horses were at the gate and the race started. People were screaming loudly. "Come on boy, go, go, come on," everyone shouting about their horse! Number 3 took the lead in the second turn and never gave up the position, followed 5 lengths behind by number 7. "Wow, what a start!" They got the winner and also the exacta. The payout was very good. They made a hundred dollars on their bets! That was the beginning of a hobby that they would enjoy for a number of years. There were more losing days than winning days! They would drive to M & T bank to cash their checks and head to the Hamburg race track. Also there was Batavia Downs, with thoroughbred racing. This track was a little far to drive, and they went to this only once a month. Raj was somewhat of a compulsive gambler and was not always careful about the wagering. If not for Chandu, some of the nights he would have ended up with big losses.

Days and months were rolling by fast and furious. Chandu had decided he would specialize in internal medicine, and Raj always wanted to be a great surgeon. They had both finished two years of training and had two more years to go. Sisters Hospital had no teaching spots, and the guys had to make decisions for future training. Mercy Hospital, in south Buffalo had openings for surgical residency and the Vets Hospital in Buffalo had medical training positions. This was the time to make a hard choice. This would mean they would work in different facilities. For the first time they would be away from each other. They had to decide how to stay close, even if they worked in different hospitals.

They started looking around and were able to find a place on Bird Avenue in Buffalo. This was very close to Michelle's home! What a fortunate coincidence, Chandu thought! Lynette lived with her mother not too far from Mercy Hospital! That was perfect for Raj! Best of both worlds, they took the apartment. This was a bigger place and they could take in two more room-mates. It so happened, two of their classmates from medical-school in India decided to come to Buffalo to start their training. Dr. Nabha and Dr. Gopal were arriving next month. They would join Chandu and Raj and share the rent, utilities, etc. Gopal was also a good cook and Nabha was very much into music and arts, etc. They knew each other very well and would get along. They were both interested in specializing in surgery as well and pur-sued the same. It didn't take long for Gopal to get hooked on harness racing!! There were more entertaining parties at the apartment. Gopal was well liked by the girls. They liked his sense of humor. Lots of Indian cooking, including pork vindaloo, lamb curry, etc! The New Year's Eve party was especially memorable. They had decorated the apartment with ribbons and bows, lots of red, white and blue! Lots of beer, Johnny Walker scotch, Black-

Velvet whiskey and Beefeater gin!! They had enough snacks to last through the night. Blasting stereo playing disco music good for dancing! By the time they watched the ball drop at Time Square on television at midnight, half of the guests would be on the floor!

Because of the different scheduling at the hospitals, Chandu and Raj had not been together much for a week or so. That night, Gopal and Nabha were both on call at Sisters, and the two buddies were alone at home for a change. They were happy to be relaxing after an exhausting week. Raj poured a glass of Johnny Walker Black Label scotch and handed it to

Chandu and made himself a drink, as well. They clinked the glasses after adding club soda and ice cubes and took a long sip!

"You know how hard it is now to get together," Raj said. "The surgery schedule is very tough and tires me out! But I enjoy it anyway. How are you doing at the Vet's Hospital?"

"Well, now I am the chief medical resident and I have added responsibilities, supervising the interns, making the call schedule, moderating mortality conferences, etc. Also making the rounds with the attendings takes up all my time." Chandu took another sip of scotch. "Hey Raj, now that you are close to Lynette's home, do you get to see her often? How is it going for you?" Chandu asked smiling.

"Actually things are moving fast, I must say! Her mother likes me very much. I have been to her house for dinner. She is a good cook. Lynette's brother is an electrical engineer and a nice guy," Raj said.

"Don't tell me things are getting serious between you two? Is it?" "I do have strong feelings for her, Chandu. I really, really like her!"

"Have you thought about what your mother might think of this?"

"No! I don't even want to think about that. But, you know she would want me to be happy and so would my brothers and sisters!" Raj continued, "I don't know how to break the news."

"Well, you have to be honest with her and tell her how much you care for Lynette," Chandu advised. "I think you should do this soon, before you commit yourself all the way."

"You are right. I am sure you will support me in my decision. I am sure, won't you? You are my closest friend, my brother!" Raj said with a choking voice.

"Yes, of course! You can count me in any time, Raj. I will do whatever it takes!" Chandu reassured Raj. They finished another glass of scotch and had some leftover chicken curry. They felt better after the talk, and they said good night and headed upstairs.

Chapter Seven

Michelle looked stunning in her dark red cardigan sweater that Chandu had given her for Valentine's day! After last night's talk with Raj about his relationship with Lynette, now it was his turn. He had been thinking long and hard about what direction he was heading. He really would want a long term relationship with Michelle, but thought about this boyfriend serving in Vietnam. What happens after he returns back home? Michelle had never brought up her boyfriend's name ever since she had been going out with Chandu! "Could she be dumping the boyfriend?" Chandu was confused! "What if the same thing happens to me," he thought, but his strong feelings for Michelle overcame those concerns. He had called Michelle on her day off and asked her to meet him at the cafeteria of the Vet's hospital for lunch. He was waiting for her near the entrance. She parked her Mustang convertible in the visitor's lot and after she spotted Chandu, she waved her hands with a big smile. Chandu gave her a big hug and a kiss, held her hand and walked to the cafeteria. They sat in silence for a minute while their eyes were brightly shining, admiring each other!

Chandu remembered the day he bought her the red cardigan. It was a cold and snowy evening when he went downtown with Raj. They went to A M & A's department store and looked for gifts for the girls. Raj bought a nice sparkling bracelet made with Austrian crystals and Chandu spotted the beautiful deep red cardigan sweater!, "She would look gorgeous in this, don't you think so, Raj?" and looked for approval. There was no argument! The very first time she wore the sweater, she had received very many compliments from her co-workers, Michelle had told him. She also got a lot of teasing from the girls.

"So, when is the big announcement coming? We expected a nice, big diamond ring for Valentine's day, Michelle!!" they asked. Michelle turned deep red and covered her face, laughing.

They both picked pizza with lots of gorp from the menu. They had ginger ale to drink. The pizza tasted good, especially after sprinkling hot pepper flakes.

"Hey, Michelle, I want to ask you something, if you don't mind." Chandu looked at her. Her eyes widened and he saw the anticipation in her looks.

"Shoot! I will answer if I know what it is!" she said.

"You never mention your boyfriend, John's name when we are together! When is he coming back home? Are you two still corresponding?" Chandu was blunt and straight forward. Michelle's smile briefly faded, and she had a serious face. She reached across the table and held Chandu's hand.

"Well, it is little more complicated, Chandu," she said in a soft voice. "My mother likes you very much and she is quite happy with our relationship. But my older brother, Robert, is still very much behind John. They practically grew up together in the same neighborhood and, in a way, they are like you and Raj, very close."

"That doesn't answer my questions. What about you? Your feelings?" Chandu pressed for an answer.

"I think we need a little more time, Chandu, to think things over!" She continued, "Then there is my Catholic religion. I don't know how that affects you and your family," she sighed. For a short minute or two, Chandu felt like lightening had struck! It never had crossed his mind that the difference in religions would be a huge hurdle.

"You know, you are right about this. We need to think long and hard before we jump into any kind of conclusion," he said. "Let's enjoy each other for now, and leave it to the Gods for the results!"

Chapter Eight

"Hey, Chandu, wc all have five days off next week. Why don't we travel somewhere nice?" Gopal asked with interest.

"That's right. We never get to take off at the same time. This would be great. I can drive my Falcon. I was thinking, maybe we can drive to Montreal. That is supposed to be a great place. From there, we can go to Quebec city and do some sight-seeing. What do you guys think?" Chandu suggested. Raj and Nabha liked the idea as well.

"O.K., then it's all set. Let me make sure the car is in good shape. I am going to take it for complete service before we leave." Chandu was excited that this would be a long trip for them.

They decided to leave early in the morning, and Chandu made sure everyone was ready by 9:00 a.m.! He always got up early before the alarm buzzer! They drove to McDonald's in the neighborhood and had a hearty breakfast consisting of egg Mcmuffin, sausages and fries! That should hold them until lunch time. After a strong cup of coffee, they headed for the Peace Bridge to Canada. Fort Erie was very close to downtown Buffalo, just across the bridge. They made sure they all had their passports for identification. Chandu was doing all the driving. They got through customs without much problem, although the Canadian officer at the border was curious as to what the guys were doing in Canada. After the usual questions, "Where were you born? How long are you staying in Canada? What are you here for?" When the officer found out these were doctors, they were let in without much hassle.

It was a nice summer day, bright and sunny. Queen E Highway, as it was called, had smooth traffic and the two lanes were moving nicely. This was the first time Chandu reached the speed limit of 70 miles per hour and was really enjoying the ride. Raj was in the front passenger seat and the other two were in the back seat. They were getting silly and started singing classical South Indian music. They stopped at a rest area after a few hours of driving and grabbed some lunch. Raj took over the driving for about an hour or so, and Chandu took over the wheel again. Gopal and Nabha had not taken their driver ed courses yet.

They drove around Toronto downtown and went to Gerard Street which was filled with Indian shops and restaurants. They went to Taj Mahal, a well known place for tandoor chicken! Eating there and seeing all the other countrymen made them think of Bangalore, India! They were very happy with the decor, the spicy chicken, mango lassi and movie music in the background!

Chandu started driving. Their destination, Montreal, was about a four hour drive. Highway 401 was great to drive. The pavement was very smooth, and the four lane highway was not very congested. The speed limit was 75 miles per hour and slowly Chandu caught up with the traffic and was driving comfortably.

They were getting close to Kingston, the next big town on the way to Montreal. Construction signs were visible in a distance, and the traffic was slowed down for a while. The four lane highway narrowed to two lanes. Chandu was following a truck that was moving at a steady pace, 80 miles per hour. There was another car behind Chandu's car, almost tailgating. The driver of that car tried to pass him and the truck that was in front of Chandu's car. As soon as he saw the car trying to pass on the left, to avoid collision, Chandu pulled to the right of the road. There was only gravel and a two feet drop off onto a field.

The next thing he noticed was, his car had flipped off the main highway onto the field with four wheels up in the air, and the engine on fire.

"Oh, God! What happened?" he screamed and looked to see if all the others were O.K. He had a few scratches and bruises, and he saw Raj was stuck between seats, but conscious and not hurt. The other two were O.K. as well! The truck driver that was in front saw what happened to Chandu's car. He came running and put out the fire with an extinguisher he had in his truck. He

pulled all the passengers out of the car and shouted, "Run, run! The car is going to blow up. Get as far away as you can."
The scene was horrible. The car was a total wreck.

"Thank God, we are all alive!! I can't believe it!!" Chandu was still shaking.

Other cars would stop by and everyone would ask, "Is anyone hurt? Do you need any help?"

They were just glad God had given them a second chance! After the police came and took reports, a priest, who was on the way to Kingston, told them to hop in the van. He said there would be a Grey coach bus to Montreal from there. They sat back and in total disbelief, sat in silence.

Chaper Nine

Chandu and Raj were almost at the end of their training and further stay in the USA would mean a change in their visa status. They both had come to this country on an exchange visitor's visa. When they would complete the post graduate training program they would have to return back to India. After they were exposed to the quality of training and the future opportunities that would open up, they already had made up their minds to stay in Buffalo to continue their careers. Raj had gotten advice from the senior attending that he would offer a position as an assistant surgeon if Raj had his green card or permanent visa. Some of other colleagues had sought help from legal firms that specialized in immigration matters.

Shapiro and Bronstein law firm was well known for this in Niagara Falls, N.Y. Raj made an appointment with attorney Shapiro to find out how to accomplish the visa status change. One of the suggestions was, Shapiro said, "If you marry an American citizen, it would make it easier to obtain a green card! If I have to start working with the immigration officials it will cost you quite a bit." He continued, "Five grand deposit initially." Raj did not expect that it was that expensive but with no guarantee!

That night Chandu and Raj talked about the problem more, with no easy solution. They could go back to India for two years and then reapply for a permanent visa. That meant they had to look for a job in India. Their classmates were already established in Bangalore, in private practice. That would be a huge disadvantage since they would have to start all over! They would never be able to use all the new skills they had learned, because the technology was still primitive in India, at that time.

"Well, let's have some scotch and think about it tomorrow," Chandu said, pouring a glass of Johnny Walker!

Now the whole future appeared very bleak and their dreams were just that!

Chapter Ten

"Hey, Chandu, what are you doing this afternoon? Let's meet at Chef's for lunch. What do you say?" Raj had some excitement in his voice.

"Sure, what's up? Everything O.K.?" Chandu quizzed.

"Yeah, yeah! I just want to discuss something with you. I will see you at noon today." He hung up the phone.

Chandu had really no clue as to what was on Raj's mind. It could be anything. Maybe he has been offered a job. Maybe Lynette and him are breaking up! Well, wait 'till lunch time, he thought.

Raj was waiting for him at the door of Chef's. He was all smiles. must be good news, Chandu thought. They sat down at the table and ordered ginger ale and meat balls and Italian hot sausage, their favorite at this restaurant. Chandu looked at Raj and asked him, "So, what's happening? You seem to be very happy! Is that the job offer?"

"No, not that! I mean, if that happens that would be great! But I want to tell you that I have made up my mind about Lynette! I am going to ask her to marry me! As you know, we have been going out for over a year now. I have gotten to like her very, very much! I really love her, Chandu! I decided it is time." Raj was very animated.

"All I can tell you, my friend, I hope you have thought about this long and hard. Hope it is not just an infatuation. Hope this has nothing to do with what the attorney Shapiro suggested! For permanent visa status, I mean. Is it?" Chandu was serious.

"No, no, no!! I really love her, Chandu. The feeling is mutual!" Raj continued. I even talked to my brother in India. I have his blessing. I only have to work on my mother. I am sure over time she will come around, as well."

Chandu felt better, and he was truly happy for his friend.

"I am extremely happy for you, Raj. So, when are you going to spring this on Lynette?"

"I am going to take her out to dinner tonight, to the Scotch & Sirloin restaurant." He reached into his coat pocket and pulled out a small jewelry box! There was a beautiful solitaire diamond ring shining!

"Lucky girl! I am sure Lynette will be very happy, Raj." Chandu handed back the box.

"Good luck and God bless you both!" Chandu shook Raj's hand and tapped his shoulder and tears rolled down his face as they both walked out.

Raj picked Lynette up from her house and they drove to the restaurant which was in Amherst, N.Y. This place was very well known for the decor, and their menu. They not only had great sea food, but also the best New York strip steak. There was a piano bar with quiet music and a fireplace with a nice mantle. When they got to the place, they noted that it was not crowded. Being a weekday, not too many customers were there. The owner knew Raj and he greeted them and ushered them to a table by the fireplace. Lighting as somewhat dim, making it more romantic! The guy at the piano was playing soft music, some classical melody!

Raj ordered two glasses of Great Western extra dry cham pagne and shrimp cocktail for appetizer. He lifted the glass and after toasting, leaned over the table and said, "I love you, Lynette, very, very much!" He continued in a soft voice, "Will you marry me? I want to spend the rest of my life with you!" Lynette was speechless for a second. She knew this might happen someday, but this was a surprise she did not anticipate. With happy tears in her eyes, she said, "Of course I will. I love you too, very much. I want to spend the rest of my life with you!" she sobbed. Raj pulled out the box and gently put the diamond ring on her ring finger.

The precious stone was sparkling by the fireplace, and the piano man seemed to be enjoying the whole scene!

They really enjoyed the dinner and their time together at the restaurant! Lynette showed the ring to the waitress, and she in turn called out the owner, Bob! They all congratulated the couple! Raj hugged Lynette and kissed her like never before, and said, "I am the happiest man on earth! Now we have to tell your mom and your brother. I can't wait to see her reaction!" Raj was full of excitement.

"I am sure Mom will be very pleased. She kind of knew this would happen, but not so soon, I think!" Lynette added, "We have to figure out the details of the big day, Raj, dear!!"

"You know, my buddy, Chandu, already knows about us and he will be with me one hundred percent in whatever I do! He is more than a friend, more like another brother!" Raj was choking on his words.

The news of Raj's engagement to Lynette was broadcast all over the hospital staff room and the nursing quarters!

The next day in the operating room while Raj was assisting, the senior attending offered him a position in the surgical department. Now, all he has to do is to contact the officials in the immigration department about his visa.

Raj and Lynette were busy planning for the big day. The wedding was going to be at St. Martin's Catholic Church in south Buffalo, which was close to her home. They decided to have a select, small group of people only for the wedding. Lynette did not have a lot of relatives. Only her mother, her brother and an aunt. She would invite some of her closest friends from work. Raj had his three buddies, and he would also invite some of the attendings he was working with. His brother from India was planning to come, but he had a problem obtaining the visa within a short time. The two were planning a honeymoon at a later date after the visa status was confirmed. Maybe they would spend time in Niagara Falls after the wedding. That was always a lover's paradise for anyone.

"Chandu, can you come with me to Tuxedo Junction to-morrow?" Raj was getting ready to rent the tuxedo. The other guys said they would pay for their own tuxedo rentals.

"Right now you are on a limited budget, Raj. We will pay for our rentals. I am sure pretty soon you will be raking in money as a surgeon!" Chandu teased him.

"Thanks, guys! I appreciate the gesture. Some day I will repay you for this in kind or coin!" Raj replied.

The next day the four of them went to Tuxedo Junction and picked out their black tuxedos. Raj tried his on and looked very handsome and debonair!

"Hey, you look like a millionaire. Remember when we landed in Buffalo how we were penniless!" Chandu chuckled.

"Gopal, you are in charge of the bachelor party," Nabha said.

"Where do you want to have the party? I know what we can do. Let's go to that burlesque place in downtown for the show and then go the Chin's which is only a block from there!" Gopal already had a plan.

"Sounds good! We will have fun. Maybe we can invite O'Hurley. He will add to the fun!" Chandu suggested. "O.K., it's all set for tomorrow evening, the day before your wedding." They were supposed to pick up their tuxedos the next morning.

Chapter Eleven

The wedding ceremony was short and sweet! Raj and Lynette exchanged vows, and Chandu was the best man. Gopal and Nabha greeted the other physicians and families at the entrance. The couple looked very happy and when the priest said, "I now pronounce you man and wife. You may now kiss the bride," Raj pushed back the bridal veil and kissed her passionately. Gopal announced that the reception would follow and would be in the American Legion Hall not too far from the church. Lynette's deceased father was a World War II veteran. The legion was kind enough to make the hall available.

After the usual wedding pictures were taken, they all headed to the hall. Everything was nicely set up. On one side was the open bar. The buffet had been set up with famous beef-on-weck and a medley of cooked vegetables, mashed potato, etc. There was a sea food appetizer and a fresh, tossed salad to follow before the main course. Every table had a bottle of red and white wine, a centerpiece of fresh cut flowers and champagne glasses ready to be filled!

The four buddies sat at the head table with their escorts! Chandu was the toastmaster, being the best man! After everyone sat down, Chandu took the microphone. "Ladies and gentlemen," he started in his actor's voice! "I want you all to wait 'till the waitress fills your champagne glass, and we will toast the newly weds," he said raising the glass.

"I have known you, Raj, for the past twelve years or more. When we left India, I promised your dear mother that we will look after each other always! I am so happy that you are fulfilling your dreams of becoming a great surgeon. Now you have a wonderful partner to share your good life with! I don't know who is luckier, you or Lynette! I will say, 'I am the luckiest to have been a brother to you, and enjoy and celebrate your success.' Here is to you, my dear friend! May you both be blessed with the very best of all that life has to offer! Good health, abundant wealth and happiness always!" He touched Raj's glass and lifted his own glass to his lips. Everyone applauded.

Chandu had a meeting with the chairman of the department of medicine at the VA medical center. Dr. Augustine really wanted to help him to change his visa status by writing supporting letters of recommendation, and also offering a staff position in the department. Also, legal help from Shapiro & Bronstein was sought. All these efforts fell short, and the immigration department was very strict in enforcing the exchange visitor status. That meant that Chandu had to leave the country and would be eligible to return in two years.

Chandu was thinking of a couple options. One was to move to Canada as an immigrant, since this was easier for someone from India, especially a fully qualified physician. He took a ride to London, Ontario, Canada, which was only an hour drive from Buffalo, N.Y. He was offered a staff position in the department of medicine.

His heart was in the field of gastroenterology in which he was trained at the VA medical center. Dr. Alvin, Chief of Division of Gastroenterology, was very impressed with Chandu's skills, and he had written in one of the recommendations, "Dr. Chandu is very well trained and he has the potential to be an outstanding specialist in the field of digestive diseases!" He had suggested to apply for further fellowship training in Royal Victoria Hospital in Montreal, Canada. Chandu had sent his application to that institution, but had to wait at least six months before he would know for sure. He talked to some of the attendings who had been in London, U.K. for advanced studies. This also looked like an option, although a temporary one at best! Like Raj, he never wanted to go the U.K. in the first place! "Well, I suppose I could spend some time in London, U.K., look for a job. If that doesn't work out, I could go back to India," Chandu thought, almost making up his mind

He discussed all this with Raj and his other buddies. Raj had received the word from immigration officials that he would be getting the green card within six months, and that was great news for him! Raj felt helpless that he had no control over what was happening to Chandu. Sure he would miss him sorely. He was the closest of friends.

Chandu had not seen Michelle in three weeks since he was so busy with his own problems. That evening, after he got home, he was alone since the other two were on call at the hospital that night. He poured himself a glass of scotch and soda and sat down at the desk. He closed his eyes for a few minutes, looking down asking for some Divine guidance! He kept thinking of the good times he had spent in Michelle's company. He remembered his graduation ceremony celebrating the completion of his internship. There was a dinner dance that followed, and Chandu and Michelle danced all night on the disco floor! She would glide with elegance, keeping up with him, and the two were the envy of the rest of the group there! The times they went out to dinner, she would insert quarters into the juke box and play her favorite tune, "When I Look Into Your Big Brown Eyes," she would sing along! He decided it was time for him to let her know about his decision. He pulled out a sheet of plain paper and started scribbling.

"Dear Michelle, This is the hardest I have felt expressing my thoughts and feelings. We have known each other for almost three years now. We both know how strongly we feel about each other. Frankly, I have never, ever met anyone that I adore and love more than you. I could never think of ever being away from you or losing you. But things now are well beyond my control, dear! I will have to leave the country and stay away for at least two years before I could come back here. Two years is an eternity, and we can't foresee our future. I wish we could. I have thought long and hard, and I believe the time has come for us to let go of each other. Just remember all the wonderful time we had together. I shall never forget those times, and you will always be in my heart. I want you to be happy always, and I hope you and your boyfriend, John, enjoy a great life together. I pray for his safe return from Vietnam and hope he will be with you soon. May God bless you and be with you always. I am not courageous enough to face you in person, nor could I see the hurt in your looks. I am placing this letter in your personal locker at the hospital tomorrow before I go to work. I remember the combination for your locker. Remember the times I had stuck notes before?

Love you always,
Chandu

He placed the letter in an envelope and sealed it after kissing it.

Chapter Twelve

Chandu made his travel plans. He would first fly to New York and take a cruise ship to Bermuda. From there travel to South Hampton, England, a seven day journey aboard the Queen E! Raj and Lynette had invited Gopal and Nabha for a farewell party at their new apartment in south Buffalo. Lynette's mother offered to cook for everybody with her help. She had prepared a nice turkey dinner with a green bean casserole, mashed potatoes and corn on the cob. There was a very nice pumpkin pie for dessert! It was a thanksgiving dinner even though three weeks early. I guess Raj felt this would be a very appropriate send off dinner for Chandu. He had no clue as to when they would see each other again. At the dinner table the mood was very somber. They raised their glasses of champagne and toasted Chandu wishing him a safe travel. Everyone knew it wouldn't be the same without Chandu.

The next day, Raj and buddies drove Chandu to the airport, and as the plane took off, there was a huge vacuum in their hearts.

"I want you to call me at least once a week or send me a letter," Raj begged Chandu before he boarded the plane. "I am going to kill you if you don't." That was his favorite expression to make a point!

"I sure will, buddy boy. Just take good care of yourself and look out for Lynette. At least you have Gopal and Nabha to fall back on if you have any problems," Chandu said as he gave a big hug to Raj.

As he sat back in his seat, tears rolled down his cheeks, and he looked out the window and saw the skyline of downtown below, wondering if and when he would return. Four years went by so fast, and the two friends had accomplished a lot. He was wondering about Michelle. What was her reaction when she found the letter he had placed in her locker? He could not face her if she had come to the airport. He had not called her to let her know when he was leaving.

The stewardess offered drinks, and he ordered a glass of scotch. "Here is to you, Raj, my friend. I will be back for sure," he said to himself under a soft breath.

When Chandu arrived in Bermuda, it was like paradise! Coming from a cold and snowy place where the sunny days were few and far between, this was a bright, sunny island surrounded by crystal clear blue waters and lots of greenery! Lots of palm trees and golf courses scattered all around the island. He had booked his stay at The Royal Imperial Resort Hotel, a very big hotel with the gorgeous view of the Atlantic ocean from the balcony. One side was the golf course and a very large swimming pool at the other end. A very nice tiki bar and a little band with steel drums and loud Caribbean music. Lots of vacationing couples sitting by the pool and enjoying fancy colorful drinks made him somewhat uneasy since he was alone! He managed to get to the bar and got a margarita and sat there sipping his drink and enjoying the steel drum beats. He had done some research about the island, and there was a very nice hospital called King Edward's Hospital and Infirmary located in the mid part of town. He thought he would visit the hospital administrator and see if there were any job opportunities. Nothing to lose, he thought!

The next day, he called for a cab, and after a few phone calls he made an appointment with the administrator. He collected all the documents, his curriculum vitae, etc., and headed to the hospital. He had a warm reception from the officials who took him around and gave a nice tour of the facility. He was impressed with how the place was equipped with modern technological equipment. The ICU, OR, and recovery areas were all well staffed. They mostly practiced U.K. style of medicine, somewhat different from the American system. There were no separate areas for doing gastrointestinal procedures. Fiberoptic endoscopes were still new and not readily available, except in large institutions in the U.S.A. or U.K. Bermuda did not have digestive disease specialists. Mostly general practitioners did most of the work including cardiology, respiratory diseases, etc.

The administrator was very impressed with the training Chandu had received, and he really wanted Chandu to start a digestive diseases clinic and establish an endoscopy unit. Chandu would be the director and be in charge of buying equipment, etc. The only problem was, he would have to wait at least six months until the funds would be made available. If there was a way for the hospital to proceed sooner, he was willing to take a chance. If that would not work out, maybe there were other opportunities when he gets to England! He sincerely thanked the hospital officials and went back to the hotel

Chapter Thirteen

The cruise ship Queen E was on the way to South Hampton. The ocean was calm for the most part, except for occasional harsh waves. The ship was full of passengers from different parts of the world. Most of the crew members were from the Philippines and spoke good English. There were full course dinners and a great buffet breakfast. There was so much food, some people would go around for seconds and thirds!! How can they eat so much, especially all three or four meals, Chandu was puzzled!

There were lots of activities on the ship, nightly entertainment with dancing and music. There were magicians, comedians, show girls and circus acts! Chandu had made friends with the ship doctor, Dr. Ambrose. He was a retired surgeon now working for the cruise ship. He was only in his early forties and enjoyed being on the sea and ocean. The life compared to his previous private practice was now free of stress and fatigue! Rarely he would have major medical emergencies. Most of the problems were related to upset stomach, diarrhea or flu like symptoms, occasional cuts or bruises requiring suturing, etc. He really enjoyed being on the ship and was very popular with the rest of the crew.

Chandu was invited to the captain's table for a special dinner that night. He was sitting next to Dr. Ambrose. The captain was a Norwegian and had a great sense of humor. "Hi, Doc! I hear you are from the States. You are a specialist in stomach problems. I have this pain in the pit of my stomach! Every time I drink anything alcoholic it gets worse! What should I do, Doc?" he asked, laughing.

"Just stick to ice water, Cap!! Hand the drink over to your co-captain!" Chandu continued, "Seriously, you should be tested. You may have an ulcer or you could have a liver problem." They decided to leave the medical field alone and enjoy the fine wine and succulent pork chops.

Chandu had finished his breakfast and was taking a walk around the deck. One attendant ran to him and said, "Dr. Ambrose needs you, Doc. He is in the operating room. Hurry." He ran back.

"I need you to assist me, Chandu," Dr. Ambrose said, scrubbing. "This gentleman has appendicitis, and we have to operate before he perforates. Go ahead and scrub and you can assist me!"

"Wow! What a chance! How often does this happen!" Chandu started scrubbing.

They completed the surgery with no problems! Another life saved!! "I will have plenty of stories to tell Raj when I call him."

The cruise ship arrived on the shores of South Hampton. When Chandu looked at the grey skies, his spirits were deflated some! "Well, this is not Bermuda!" he thought as he set his foot on land.

"May I see your passport, sir?" the customs officer asked. He looked at it for a few minutes and asked, "So, you are a doctor! What are you going to do here?"

"I am going to look for work. Maybe for some additional training," he continued. "For now I need a visitor's visa for six months, sir!"

"That's all you are going to get, doctor. Good luck," the officer said as he stamped the passport.

"Where is the nearest inn I can stay here in South Hampton?" he asked the officer.

"There is the West Winchester Inn, about three miles from here. It is a nice place, very reasonable daily rates and good meals!" He said, "Also there are a bunch of old folks that live there. Maybe they could use a doctor!" He was joking as he laughed. "What part of India are you from? I know Bombay, I have been to Calcutta, New Delhi! You name it, I have been there," he was boasting as if he knew more about India than Chandu did!

"I am from Bangalore. Have you heard of Bangalore torpedoes?" Chandu quizzed him.

"Of course I have. I spent nearly five years working in the Viceroy's office. I love Indian food, that curry stuff!" He really wanted to impress Chandu.

"Well, that's good, officer! I will be on my way now. I need to convert some American dollars to sterling. Where is the exchange?"

"Right in this building. You know our pound costs more than your dollar bill! You know that, right?" He was so proud.

"Yes, sir, I believe two dollars per pound. But I have no choice." He started to walk towards the exchange. He converted a couple of hundred dollar bills and hailed a taxicab. "Hi, please take me to West Winchester Inn, driver," he said to the driver as he slid into the back seat. "What is the temperature like today?" Chandu felt somewhat cold.

"Maybe twenty degrees Celsius! That is around fifty five degrees for you folks from the States! We have had lots of bloody rainy days here! A parasol is a must."

"I guess I have to buy an umbrella soon," Chandu finished.

The cab arrived at the inn, which looked very old fashioned to him. Not the Holiday Inn, he thought, but with limited budget this would do for now.

Chapter Fourteen

It had been almost a week since Chandu had arrived in U.K. The stay at the inn was not very comfortable. Nights were cold and the heater in the room was coin operated! The shillings that were needed to keep the heater operating kept mounting by the day. The meals were very bland! He was getting sick of having fish and eggs for breakfast everyday. Most of the time he was sitting alone at the table. He tried to strike a conversation with some old folks that came down to eat, but they were never friendly, not like the gabby Americans!! The only thing they talked about was the weather and their dogs! There was a TV room and the folks were busy watching cricket or rugby or some silly British slapstick comedy hour with dry sense of humor! This was not at all appealing to Chandu. He would get on the 'tube,' subway to London and did some sightseeing, London Bridge, Buckingham Palace, Picadilly Square, Trafalgur, lots of statues, everywhere!! He saw lots of his fellow Indians doing all kinds of jobs, janitors, cab drivers, shoe shiners, and bus boys. This was different from the states where mostly he ran into Indian doctors, engineers, professors and attorneys! He had joined the British Medical Council in the hope of getting a specialist job in the hospital. He was only offered some junior position in a totally unrelated specialty such as dermatology or psychiatry!! "That's not for me! Even if I have to go without a job here in U.K.," he thought.

He got back to the inn that afternoon and got a drink of scotch from the bar and sat down to watch the news in the TV room.

"Doctor, Doctor C, there is a gentleman having a hard time breathing. Could you come and check him please?" the inn's owner shouted at Chandu. Chandu grabbed his doctor's bag that was in his room and rushed to see Sir Roberts in room 212. Mr.

Roberts was a World War II veteran, about 75 years of age. He was a smoker and coughed frequently whenever he would come down to the TV room.

"You should quit smoking, Sir Roberts!! You can die of cancer of the lung!!" Chandu advised him several times, but the advice fell on deaf ears!

Roberts looked somewhat blue and was very short of breath. His pulse was weak but rapid and irregular. Chandu looked at his legs and the calf muscles were tender to touch, especially on one side. He had weak pulses in the ankles. After he listened to the lung sounds and heart, he knew Mr. Roberts had blood clots in his lungs! He asked the owner to call for an ambulance and said he would call the hospital.

The ambulance was there within minutes and the medics put an oxygen mask over Robert's nose. After getting him on a gurney, they transferred him to the ambulance. They had an intravenous line started already, and the heart monitor was on. Chandu could see that the heartbeats were irregular and fast. The condition was atrial fibrillation. This would confirm his impression of what was happening. Two hours later he received a call from the hospital emergency room.

"Dr. Grant wants to talk to you, Dr. Chandu," the nurse said.

"Hello, is this Dr. Chandu? I just wanted to call you and tell you that your diagnosis of blood clot in the lung was right on! I must congratulate you. We confirmed it by doing a lung scan, and we started him on blood thinners! You saved his life. Thank you for your help." Dr. Grant hung up the phone. Chandu was very happy that he could make the correct diagnosis just by checking Sir Roberts at his bedside. All the training in the states had paid off! Ten days later, Sir Roberts was back at the inn, feeling much better. When he saw Chandu he shook his hand and said, "You are a genius, Dr. C! You saved my life. My cardiologist said the same thing! I owe you a drink! Here, this is for you!" and he handed him a bottle of J & B scotch!!

"You shouldn't have, Sir Roberts. Thanks very much. I am going to enjoy this. Thanks again! Stay well!" Chandu smiled.

Now Chandu had a friend who sat at the same table for breakfast and dinner. Roberts shared his war stories everyday!

Chandu was looking through the classified ads in the London Times and spotted an ad looking for a chief medical officer in Al Khobar, Saudi Arabia, a hospital affiliated with Aramco. They were particularly looking for a specialist trained in America. It would be a two year contract, and the hospital would pay for room and board and a generous salary was included. No taxes!!

"I can't lose anything," Chandu thought. "Let me apply and hope for the best!" He completed the necessary documents and went to the post office and sent it by express mail.

He was on the way back from the post office and as he was walking he spotted a sign that said, "Famous Clairvoyant, Madame Francesca. Come find out what's in your future!" Chandu always had liked astrology and the paranormal powers some possess. He remembered the palmistry predictions he and Raj heard while in Madras, India. Something made him walk to the door of this clairvoyant. Madame Francesca was in her fifties, grey hair and green eyes. She had an unusual aura with a reassuring smile. She greeted Chandu, "Hello there. Looks like you could use some help! I can see that you are someone with faith! Come in and I can see what's in store for you," she said with confidence. "I don't charge much. Just ten pounds for an hour's worth of reading."

Chandu sat down across from her and said, "O.K.. What do you want me to do?"

Madame reached out and took his right hand and held it for a few minutes. Then she stared at the ceiling and closed her eyes for a second or two. "I see a lot of travel in your future! You will be going back to India. Very soon you will meet a foreign man who is very important in the medical field. He is tall, has grey hair and a very fair complexion. He will offer you a job in an institution near your city. You will have a big place to live. You will be very much liked, but I see that you will not stay there for long! At the most six months or so!" she continued. "I see you traveling to another country and you will be staying at a place near a large body of water and I see lots of sand around! You will be taking care of very important, wealthy people!! You will make good money!! You will be away from your family and friends for some time."

"What about my personal life? Am I going to settle down?" Chandu was curious.

"You will find happiness, but you have to wait a while before this can happen," she said, looking at Chandu's eyes. "You are going to run into some tough times. But it will all work out in the end," she finished. Madame continued talking to Chandu, asking him what his plans were. Chandu told her how difficult it had been for him to find a job in the U. K. She reassured him that going back to India was the right choice at this time, and things would work out.

Chandu felt a sense of relief, and after paying Madame Francesca, he said goodbye to her and headed back to the inn.

He decided to start making travel plans the following week.

He had to call Raj and find out how things were between him and Lynette and their married life!

Chapter Fifteen

Raj had a busy day at the hospital. He had to assist the senior surgeon in five major surgical procedures, and he had his own three cases to work on. Thank God, he had a hearty breakfast at home. Lynette made sure he had a good most important meal of the day! He had late afternoon office hours and when he came to the office, Chris, his receptionist, said, "Doctor, your close friend, Chandu, called from the U.K. He wants you to call him."

Raj had been thinking about him and wondering what was going on.

"Let me get on the phone, Chris! Don't interrupt if any other calls come in! O.K." and he dialed the long distance number.

"Hello, this is Dr. Chandu."

"Hey, this is Raj! How the hell are you? Are you still alive?"

"Of course I am, boy! I just want to tell you that I have decided to go back to India and maybe work there if I can find a decent job!" He continued, "I have had no offers here in London. They want me to work in psychiatry or dermatology, and I am a trained specialist in gastroenterology. Why would I work in those stupid fields! You know, six months went fast and all I have done is some sightseeing!" he laughed. "I think it's time for me to eat some good home cooking. By the way, how are you guys doing? Lynette and you, any progress?"

"We've been very busy decorating and furnishing our new place," Raj continued, "I have been very busy with surgeries, and I have no time for too much relaxation. I told Lynette to quit work so that she can take care of the home front!"

"Well, Raj, take some time off if you can and you should take that honeymoon you owe her!!" Chandu reminded him.

"You know, I have been thinking of that, as well. I want to surprise her! I am thinking Aruba!" Raj said.

"That's great. You do that! I am leaving the day after to-morrow, flying to Frankfurt and then on to Bombay and Banga-lore. Wish me luck, buddy! I am certainly going to miss you," Chandu sighed. "I will be in touch whenever I can, and I want you to do the same! O.K?"

"I will be praying for you. Hope you can come back to the U.S.A. soon. Bon voyage and good luck." Raj was sobbing! Chris looked at him and she could see the tear drops on his cheeks.

"You know, I am going to take off now Chris. Things are quiet and I don't think we have any more patients to see today," Raj said. "I might as well surprise my wife and take her out to dinner!"

"That sounds good. Maybe you could relax a little after your call from your dear friend." Chris started collecting the mail and keys.

"See you tomorrow. We will start the office early. I don't have any surgery scheduled unless any emergency comes up, you know." Raj changed to his jacket and walked out the door.

Lynette was very surprised to see him come home early for a change! "Wow, you are early! What happened?" she asked Raj smiling.

"I got a call from my buddy, Chandu, from London today. He will be going back to India the day after tomorrow. I guess he didn't have any luck finding a decent job in the U.K."

"Was he O.K.? How did he sound?" Lynette was curious.

"He was not too happy, but you know him! He is always optimistic! I am sure he will find a good job in India, soon." Raj gave Lynette an affectionate kiss on her lips. He continued, "Hope you didn't cook for us. Let's go out to dinner I always wanted to go to Orchard Downs. They have great food, steak or seafood. Get ready and I will call for reservations. O.K., honey?" Raj stroked her blonde hair. Lynette felt good that it was one of those rare days with dinner out! A couple of times when they were out having dinner, phone calls would interfere with their time alone. They had to rush through, and he would disappear back into the hospital operating room! She prayed for peace and quiet this time!

They drove to Orchard Downs restaurant and the place was packed as usual. Thank God for the reservation! They got a nice table. He ordered a couple glasses of champagne. Grace, the waitress, handed them the menu. "The special of the day is a six ounce steak and lobster tail," she said, "for ten ninety five! For appetizers, I recommend a combo plate of stuffed banana peppers, shrimp tempura, and fried vegetables." That sounded very good!

"We will go for the special, Grace," Raj said, "also the combo plate, O.K.? Thanks," he said as she filled the two glasses of champagne.

"Here is to us and our buddy, Chandu." Raj lifted his glass and they clinked the glasses!

Appetizers and the dinner that followed were excellent.

"I am so glad we came here! Everyone always raved about this place and their food and decor. Now I can see why!" Raj said.

Chapter Sixteen

Chandu was on the way to Heathrow airport in a taxicab, and his flight was to leave at 11:30 p.m. to Frankfurt, Germany. After clearing customs, he boarded the plane. After he sat down a very strange feeling came over him. For the first time in almost five years he felt very lonely and empty. As he looked out the window, he wondered whether he would ever be back to the U.S. What if the Indian government gave him a hard time? He thought of what Madame Francesca had predicted. Maybe there was hope.

"What do you want to drink, Sir?, the pretty blonde stewardess was asking. "Scotch and soda, please," Chandu answered.

"Where are you headed?" the passenger sitting next to him enquired trying to break the ice. "I am Jim Turner, and I am going to India. I assume you are from India, right?"

"Yes, Jim, I am from Bangalore, India. That is south India," Chandu continued. "Have you ever been in India before?"

"No, this will be my first time. I am going to New Delhi on an assignment. I work for a financial firm," Jim said. Drinks arrived and they both had scotch in their glasses.

"Cheers! Jim, I am sure you will have a great time in New Delhi. Hope you like spicy foods! One thing you'll have to get used to is the population! It's nothing like you have ever seen!! It will be a shocker, all those people, all the vehicles and animals on the street! But it's very colorful! You will get used to it." Chandu laughed.

"What about the language? Is that a problem?" Jim asked.

"No, not at all! Practically everyone speaks English! That is Royal English!! We were trained by the British, you know!"

"Well, that is good to know. Are you going for a visit or do you live there, Chandu?" Jim was curious.

Chandu told him the story of how he ended up in the states and about his training, etc.

"So, you are a specialist! Tell me, Doc what can I do to lose weight?" Jim was serious.

"Well, Jim! There is no magic pill as of now! It is all in moderation, portion control!" Chandu continued, "less fatty and greasy foods and more of good proteins. Plenty of fresh fruits and green veggies. If you combine this with regular walking at least four to five times a week, I think anyone can stay fit!" Chandu came across very authoritative!

Jim just nodded his head. They had a second glass of scotch and waited for the food.

Chandu was happy to have someone to chat with, especially an American. He missed all his patients and his attending physicians. He was wondering about Raj. He was happy that Raj could get his green card and stay in Buffalo.

There was a Hitchcock movie being shown, and Chandu enjoyed the movie. He was into detective novels, and he had read most of the Perry Mason classics. Raj and he always watched the Perry Mason show that was on the television every week.

After the movie, the lights were dimmed and the stewardess brought the blankets. "We will be serving breakfast in about three hours!" she said.

"We just ate our dinner!! I might skip the next meal," Chandu mumbled.

It was almost 5:30 in the morning when the plane touched down at the Frankfurt airport. They both got out of the plane and headed to the washrooms.

"Jim, how about a cup of coffee and some breakfast?" Chandu asked.

"O.K.! That sounds good. Let's find a coffee bar;" Jim replied. They were able to find a beverage bar and had a light breakfast and a good cup of coffee.

"So, Doc, do you have any plans? What will you be doing in India?"

"First thing I am going to do is catch up on my sleep, Jim!! And I will enjoy my mother's good home cooked meals!! I just want to relax for a couple of weeks, visit some of my old friends and classmates if I can find them! It is almost five years since I left and I am not sure who is still in Bangalore!" Chandu was somewhat emotional.

"I can appreciate that, Doc. A lot of things can happen in five years! The only thing I hope for is that you will come back to America. We need more like you, Doc! I sincerely mean it," Jim said, patting Chandu on his shoulder. It was time to get back to board the aircraft again, and they went through the customs once more in the middle of tight security to their gates. The next destination was New Delhi, and they would arrive there early morning. It was still dark when the plane landed in New Delhi. After they got off, they had to go through customs and immigration.

"Take care, Doc. Hope to see you soon," Jim said to Chandu while shaking his hand. "I guess I have to stand in a separate line. Goodbye!" He stepped out to join a different line.

Chandu got all his baggage, went through customs. The customs officer looked at him with a smile and said, "I see you have two bottles of scotch! You are only allowed to have one! I will take that one, and then you don't have to open your suitcase. I am sure you have some electronic goods that you need to pay a duty fee." Chandu didn't want to argue with the officer. He handed him the bottle of scotch and walked out without having to open the suitcase!

He went to the washroom, brushed his teeth and used the electric shaver. He felt very exhausted from the long journey and needed to have a fresh cup of coffee. There was a little café near the domestic airline window. He ordered a hot cup of coffee and some snacks for breakfast. That felt good and now the waiting began for the ticket counter to open for the domestic flight to Bangalore. The flight was scheduled to leave abound 7:30 a.m. There was some mechanical problem with the aircraft and there was a two hour delay till the problem was fixed!

In two hours Chandu would be back home!

He walked out of the baggage claim area and saw several hundred people waiting to greet their arrivals.

"Here you are, Chandu. Chandu! Welcome back home! You look great! You look like an American!!" Chandu's sister, Shilpa grabbed him and gave him a big hug. He looked around and all his four brothers and his sister-in-law were standing, waving!! He was looking for his mom and dad, and they were in the back row with tears flowing down their cheeks. Chandu ran to them and gave them a long hug and he couldn't control sobbing. All around there were tears of joy!!

"I am glad you made it back safe," Chandu's father continued. "You can rest up after a long journey. Your mother has prepared a very good lunch for you. Your cousins and uncles are all coming." He was very excited.

"You look like you have lost weight! Didn't they feed you in America?" his mother asked Chandu. "I will make sure that you eat right. Let's go." They all got in the rental van, and his brother, Ramu, said to the driver, "Let's take the doctor home! Home, sweet home.!"

Chapter Seventeen

Lynette was waiting for Raj to come home. Earlier she had received a call from Chandu.

"Hi, Hon! I am home a little sooner than I thought." Raj kissed her soon after he entered the house. "How was your day? Did the new dishwasher guy show up?" Raj enquired.

"Yup, that is all done now. It works fine. Thank God the dishes come out nice and clean! By the way, you had a call from India earlier, from Chandu! He wants you to call him. He may have some good news! But he didn't tell me. He wants to tell you first, I guess!" Lynette smiled.

"O.K., maybe I'll have my glass of scotch now, and I can talk to him!" Lynette poured him a glass of scotch with soda water.

"Hello, this is Raj calling from America! Is Chandu there, please?"

"Hold on, hold on," a young, soft voice said at the other end. I will get him!"

"Hey! This is you, Raj! I was waiting for your call! How are you? Hope all is well with you two love birds!!" Chandu said, laughing.

"We are fine, both of us! Soon maybe all three of us!" Raj said, teasingly.

"Is that so? I know you got back from your honeymoon about a month ago!! I guess that worked!! Congratulations, buddy. I am very, very happy for you guys! When is the due date?"

"The doctor says October, third week. Pray for us. Maybe it will be a boy!" Raj was excited. "Tell me about your good news, Chandu."

"Well, my brother's friend knew this medical director of a T.B. sanitarium in Andhra Pradesh, and he is looking to hire a specialist, preferably one trained in America. I guess he has some time at the airport here in Bangalore on his way to New Delhi. He wants to meet me and interview me at the airport!"

"That really sounds great! If you are offered a job, will you take it?" "At this stage, I will take anything!" Chandu was emphatic!

"Good luck and let me know what happens, and take care. We'll talk again." Raj said goodbye as he hung up the phone.

"Don't forget to say your prayers!" Chandu's dad was also doing the special prayers.

"You still have plenty of time to get to the airport. I have prepared masala dosa, your favorite breakfast dish with nice, hot coriander chutney." His mother continued, "I want to make sure you don't go hungry! We are not sure how long your interview will last."

Chandu was very happy to oblige. After eating, he collected all the papers, diplomas, and recommendation letters and placed them in his briefcase. The taxicab driver arrived on time. He got into the car and waved goodbye to his parents. "I will see you later. Keep praying! Hope everything works out. I will let you know soon. Bye!!"

When he got to the conference room at the airport, he looked at his watch and he was at least half an hour early. He was waiting for a tall foreign figure! There he was, a tall gentleman with gray hair and glasses. He had a very fair complexion with some freckles on his face and arms.

"Wow! That clairvoyant, Madame Francesca, was right on the money," he thought!

"Hello, you must be Dr. Chandu! I am Dr. Fred Muller, the medical director at the sanitarium. Great to see you! I have heard a lot about you from your brother's friend. It is all good!!" He laughed as he shook Chandu's hand. The grip was very firm!

"Thank you for meeting me here, Dr. Muller. I really appreciate this. I am really looking forward to working with you in Arogyavaram Sanitarium. Here, let me give you these documents for you to review. If you need anything else, I will be glad to furnish that for you!" Chandu sounded very sincere and eager.

Dr. Muller glanced at the documents for a few minutes and looked impressed. "Well, when can you start? We are really looking for a well trained internist, specialist in our facility. I will be going back the end of the week after my Delhi visit. Can you join next Monday? Or is this too short a notice for you?" Dr. Muller enquired.

"I don't even have to think about it, Dr. Muller!! I can start next Monday. There is a bus service that goes to Nellore, and I guess there is a shuttle bus service from there to Arogyavaram! I can take that!!"

"Good, very good!! You are going to have your own quarters, and you will also have a cook and a housekeeper!" Dr. Muller continued, "I am not sure if you can cook! This cook is a young fellow and you will like him. Oh, you will be compensated handsomely, as well, and you will have two week's paid vacation. Hope this is O.K. with you!"

Chandu thanked his stars, shook Dr. Muller's hand, and said, "I can't thank you enough, Dr. Muller! I will make sure you are not disappointed. I certainly want to contribute to the best care of your patients! Thanks again. I will see you Monday."

"You know it has almost been two months since Chandu has been working in India for that Swedish medical director! I guess he likes it there. I got a letter from him today, and he has written something funny!" Raj was talking to Lynette as they were having their dinner. "Apparently his father came to visit him in Arogyavaram. You know Chandu has a big place, a personal cook and a housekeeper, right? As you know, we are supposed to be purely vegetarians! Of course we were the exceptions, since we were doctors! Apparently this cook prepared two or three dishes. One of them was curried lamb! By mistake, Chandu's father was served the lamb! He had taken a bite of it before Chandu realized this! So, he quickly grabs the food and placed it on his plate!! I guess he apologized for the mishap profusely! Of course his father is such a gentleman, he just laughs and only says, "I will always remember this, Chandu!! Just don't tell your mother!! Is this funny or what!" Raj was laughing. Lynette joined him in laughter and kissed Raj on his lips.

"How are you feeling, sweety? You are really looking great. How is that baby of ours? I bet he is making all kinds of moves, right?" Raj put his hand over her pregnant belly and gently rubbed it!! He could feel the baby's kick!! "Wow, he just kicked me!! I guess he'll be a football player!"

Lynette was very happy. "He sure is very active. I have to go see the obstetrician tomorrow for a checkup. Hope all will be O.K. You are coming home late tomorrow you said, right?"

"Yeah! I have to attend the quarterly staff meeting at the hospital. Most boring meeting! But, as an attending, I must go," Raj was confessing!

"I am going to bed now, honey. Kind of tired! See you up-stairs." Lynette headed up.

Raj sat in the living room watching T.V. He liked to watch 'Gun Smoke'. He was thinking about Batavia Downs! He had not been to the race track in some time.

Dr. Barone had asked him that morning, "Hey, Raj, to-morrow my horse is running in the sixth race. He has a great chance to win! Want to come?"

Raj knew he had to skip the staff meeting to go to the races! "Well, Lynette knows I am going to come home late. It will be nice to make some extra money with the baby coming and all." He had made up his mind.

Chapter Eighteen

"You have two registered letters today, Sir. They look very important." Chandu's housekeeper handed him the envelopes. One had a Canadian address and the other one was from Saudi Arabia! His heart started pounding.

"Could this be the big break I've been waiting for? The one that Madame Francesca had predicted!" Chandu opened the letter from Canada. This was from the Royal Victoria Hospital in Montreal, with an offer for a fellowship in gastroenterology for two years with a generous salary. He remembered applying for the position before he left Buffalo.

He read the letter from Saudi Arabia. They were offering a Chief Internist position at As-Salama Hospital in Al Khobar near Dharan. The offer was very attractive. It would be a two year contract with free boarding and lodging and a tax-free salary!!

He remembered his dad telling him, "Chandu, you need to help finance your sister's wedding. If all of you kids pitch in, she can have a nice wedding! It looks like we may have a suitable boy for her, an engineer! Electronics, I think." There were plans underway already!

Chandu also knew about the vacant land the family had owned for a very long time in a small town near Bangalore. His dad's wish was to build a small house and have a nice flower garden! Maybe a few fruit trees!! He poured himself a glass of scotch with soda water and sat on the front porch. It was a beautiful, peaceful evening with a gorgeous sunset! His thoughts went back to Madame Francesca! She had told him about a large body of water visible from his living quarters and about the financial good fortune! He could help with his sister's wedding plans and also make his dad's lifetime dream come true, having his own place with a little garden! Ever since his retirement from government service, he had used all of his resources in the education of all his kids. He was very proud of the fact that everyone of his children had accomplished what he couldn't, since his father did not have the financial capabilities.

Two engineers, one lawyer, one doctor and two teachers!! "What more can I ask for," his father would say, proud as a peacock!!

Chandu went in the house, stood in front of God Srinivas's picture and closed his eyes muttering prayers asking for guidance. It would be Saudi Arabia for sure!! He had to inform Dr. Muller in the morning.

"Dr. Muller, I want to talk to you about some new developments. I want to discuss them with you. When is the best time for you?" Chandu asked.

"Chandu, why don't you come to dinner tonight at our place. My wife is a good cook. You know we are Swedish. Our food may be a little bland for you! But I will have her prepare something you might like. Do you care for Swedish meatballs? I will have her make it a little spicy!"

"That sounds great, Dr. Muller. I will see you tonight." Chandu wanted to explain in person about his decision to go to Saudi Arabia.

When he went to Dr. Muller's bungalow, surrounded by a beautiful English garden filled with tulips of all different brilliant colors, Chandu was very impressed! On one side of the walkway, rosebushes adorned the area. The fragrance of red roses permeated the air. There was a swingset on the front porch. He went to the door and rang the bell.

He could hear a dog bark. He always liked dogs. Memories of his childhood flashed before him. He was remembering Tommy, a mixed breed dog, a very handsome one with a nice brown coat. Chandu was about six years old and they lived in a small village, when his dad started to work for the federal government. The house was big and old and was built with stones, brick and mud! There was a nice backyard surrounded by tall trees. There was an old banyan tree and a tree full of tamarind. His dad had a nice vegetable garden that had green beans, eggplants and a large area filled with herbs, cilantro, dill, mint, all nice and fresh!

On one side of the house was a barn with a cow, a real milking cow! Everyday they had fresh milk and fresh vegetables from the garden. Life was so peaceful and simple then, Chandu thought! He remembered the dreadful day Tommy lost his life. In the very early morning hours they heard a lot of growling and barking in the backyard. Dad and the housekeeper rushed to the back yard to see what was happening. It was like a nightmare. Tommy was fighting off a cheetah that was trying to attack the cow in the barn. He did succeed in fending off the vicious attack, but suffered fatal injuries during the fight. Poor Tommy didn't survive, but the cow was safe. This, Chandu never forgot. What a sacrifice. What a courageous dog!

Mrs. Muller answered the doorbell. "Come in, Dr. Chandu. He will be right down." Lucy Muller was a very attractive blonde, tall and very soft spoken. She looked very dignified.

"So, Dr. Chandu, what's on your mind? Shoot!" Dr. Muller smiled.

"I have an offer to work for an ARAMCO Hospital in Saudi Arabia, Dr. Muller. I also have a fellowship position offer from Montreal, Canada. I will be head of the department of medicine if I go to Saudi Arabia. Apparently it is a two hundred bed hospital and has a large outpatient clinic. Their usual clients are British and French families of oil refinery workers. They also have other nationalities as well. They want to upgrade their cardiac care unit and make it modern," Chandu continued with some excitement. "I think it will be very challenging for me! What do you think?"

"Well, that really sounds great! The whole middle east area is very politically unstable. That concerns me, Chandu."

"I know that. But right now conditions are stable. I am not afraid. I like to see new places and meet new people! I have to get used to their strict culture." Chandu went on to say the real reason he chose to take this offer.

"Dr. Muller, you have met my father when he came to visit me. I have this sister and her wedding plans are underway. My father needs financial help. Then, there is this vacant land our family owns near Bangalore. My father's dream is to build a small house with a nice little garden. I think I can help with these, God willing!"

"I think you have made the right decision, Chandu! Your father will be very proud of you boys! When do you have to leave?"

"They have given me two weeks to obtain my visa from the Saudi embassy. I will have to go to Bombay for that. So, I request you to release me by the end of the week. I really appreciate it. I know this is kind of a very short notice! But you can see that they didn't give me much time," Chandu apologized.

"That will be fine, Chandu. I have really enjoyed having you work at the sanitarium. In a short three months you have already proved yourself to be a highly trained specialist. I wish you nothing but the best!! Good luck to you! Now let's eat!"

Chapter Nineteen

It was quite an emotional night at Chandu's. The next morning he would be on his way to Saudi Arabia.

"It feels like you just got here after nearly five years. You are going away again. We are going to miss you very much here. We all like the unusual experience you are going to have to face while there, but we wish you the very best!" Chandu's father was very emotional.

"You have to take care of your health. I know you are a doctor, but you neglect to take care!" Ramu, his older brother cautioned.

"I will be O.K. Don't worry about me. If I don't like it there, I can always quit and come home!" Chandu assured.

His sister, Shilpa, had been crying the whole day. "You are doing this for me and how can I ever thank you? You are doing this for the family! I am sure God will bless you with lots of wealth and happiness."

His mother was mostly silent and anyone could see the hurt in her face. "I have prepared some of your favorite snacks. At least that will last a couple of weeks," she said while packing the small plastic bags.

"I hope the customs officers don't confiscate this, Mother!" Chandu laughed.

The brothers stayed up a little late and celebrated with a glass of scotch that Chandu had brought from America!

He got up early in the morning after he heard his father saying prayers. He could smell the sandalwood incense burning in the little God house. Oil lamps were lit and jasmine flowers were on the ivory statuettes of Gods!

"Come and pray before you have your breakfast," his father said to Chandu. He silently said his prayers and kneeled down on the floor at his father's feet. He could not control the tears running down his cheeks. His father just lifted Chandu after stroking his head gently. He had tears in his eyes as well.

The whole family wanted to be at the airport to say farewell. After he went through the gates, Chandu looked back as everyone of his family members were waving their hands high up in the air! He waved back to them and headed to the jumbo jet that was ready to take off!

The PanAm 747 landed at the Dahran International Airport on time. Just as the plane was getting closer to the ground, Chandu could only see a huge sandy desert with scattered oil refineries in sight. The land looked pretty much void of any greeneries that he was used to seeing while in India. Few stone buildings were scattered here and there. After he cleared customs he was greeted by a gentleman holding up A sign, "Dr. Chandu — Al Khobar."

Chandu walked to him and said, "I am Dr. Chandu. Are you the driver?"

"Yes, doctor," the driver said with a distinct Arabic accent! All around people were talking in Arabic language! Chandu felt strange!

"I will be taking you to the hospital, Doctor. The medical director is waiting there. I will first take you to the quarters. You can freshen up and then come to the hospital. Actually you just enter the building through the back door." The driver took the luggage and walked to the parking lot. Chandu walked out of the airport and suddenly felt like he was in an oven!! The temperature outside was 123 degrees, and this was a shocker!! India was hot but not this hot he thought!

He got into the Mercedes Benz which was spacious and air conditioned! Thank God! "Is it always this hot, Ali?" he asked the driver.

"This month has been. Also, we have to watch for the sand storms," Ali cautioned. "We may run into one on the way. All we do is pull to the side and wait until it passes. Don't be scared! We are used to this." He was reassuring.

"This is all new to me! You know what you are doing. I trust you." Chandu settled down.

The hospital was about fifteen miles from the airport.

Fortunately there was no sand storm that morning. Chandu thanked his Stars! After he got up to the quarters he was impressed with the view from the balcony. He could see the blue waters of the gulf for miles and miles. This was exactly what Madame Francesca had predicted! The place was spacious and was fully air conditioned.

After he shaved and showered, he walked through the door connecting to the hospital building. It only took a short five minute walk, but he was perspiring and was having trouble breathing the very hot air!

He went to the director's office and was greeted by a middle eastern gentleman. He was in his mid forties, Chandu guessed.

"Welcome, welcome to Khobar, Dr. Chandu! I will take you around and give you a tour of the hospital and also introduce you to some of the other staff members. You will meet some doctors trained in America. But I think you are the only Indian doctor!" he laughed and continued, "Let's start visiting our out-patient department first.

"Hi! I am Dr. Manukian and I am the chief of surgery! I am glad that you are here heading the department of medicine. I was trained in Baltimore, Johns Hopkins. I understand you are a GI specialist and trained in Buffalo, N.Y. I had some friends in Buffalo working at the Millard Fillmore Hospital. I don't know where they are now."

"I am happy to meet someone from the states Dr. Manukian."

"Oh, just call me Manuk," he laughed. "I want to tell you the routine here. As you have noticed we are all kind of like prisoners! Practically everything shuts down between noon and four in the afternoon. That is their prayer time. Also, let me tell you, you are not allowed to go out with girls! No dating Saudi women, Chandu! There is no outdoor café or bar you can go to. Another thing, if you are in a car and it's 12 noon, the driver stops and gets out of the car, puts his prayer rug on the sand and starts praying! You may have to sit inside until he is done."

"Well, I guess I have to get used to all these new restrictions! I have no choice, do I?" Chandu sighed.

"Friday is our day off. No clinic. Thursday night is poker night. All the staff and the administrator get in on the action starting around eight o'clock. Usually we play until early morning. This is for real money! I hope you like poker." Manuk was encouraging.

"I do like poker. I can pick up! I need a little bit of luck!" Chandu was happy about some form of entertainment. The doctors were allowed to keep alcohol in their rooms, but not take it outside. They had to save the empty containers for the Saudi housekeepers to dispose!

The clinics were interesting. All the women wore the burkah and veil over their faces. Men wore the traditional garb with a headdress. Most of the Saudi men came to the clinic with four or five wives, sometimes with children following!

Chandu had the assistance of a nurse/interpreter while gathering their physical complaints and problems. Most of the men were mostly concerned with their sexual performance, especially having to satisfy multiple wives! Lots of testosterone injections!! They were happy with the results!

Most of the women that sought help were of foreign descent, German, British and French women.

"I guess it must be very difficult to live under these strict rules. How do you manage?" Chandu asked one British lady.

"That's why we need antidepressants, doctor!! My husband's contract runs out at the end of the year. I can't wait to get back to London."

"I don't blame you! What impresses me here is the fact that you ladies come in fully covered, and when you get up on the exam table you are almost all ready for the beach!" Chandu chuckled. The lady joined in the laughter as well.

"You know this is the only chance we get to show ourselves! We can't wander around the streets with our short skirts, doctor. They will put us away for good, somewhere underground just like they did to one of your other doctors. He was from Egypt."

Chandu was curious. "Why, what happened? What did he do?"

"Well, I guess he was caught on the street with a nurse and they were at a café having tea! Next thing we found out, the doctor disappeared from the scene! Even today no one knows where he is! As for the poor nurse, she was deported back to Lebanon."

"Oh my God." Chandu was horrified of the thought. He had to watch himself!!

The next day, Chandu was having a conversation with Manuk.

"You know, Manuk, how are we able to get all the alcoholic drinks when they usually get confiscated if seen by the police?"

"Chandu, you know that customs' officer, Amir Bin Bandar? Most of the confiscated alcohol ends up at his place! You will have to be nice to him. He is the one to give clearance when you are ready to leave the country." Manuk was serious.

It was almost 2:00 a.m. and Chandu was sound asleep! There was a Gentle knock on the door. Who could this be at this hour?

"Doctor, Doctor Chandu, we have an emergency. We have to make a house call. Please get your bag." That was the voice of the nursing director, Rashmi!

"What is wrong? Who is sick?" Chandu was anxious. "Amir Bin Bandar. You know. The customs officer!"

"Oh, him!! O.K. Make sure you have ten percent dextrose and some intravenous vitamin B-1!" Chandu already could guess the problem.

They got in the Mercedes Benz and driver Ali drove to the big palatial home of Amir Bin Bandar. As soon as they entered the huge room, he was struck by the enormity of the fully decorated place. The ceiling was full of crystal chandeliers. The floor had wall to wall rich Persian rugs, and beautiful Victorian-style furnishings were all neatly scattered. On one of the plush couches there was Amir, passed out, halfway on to the floor and his hand holding a Beefeater gin bottle, mostly empty except for a few drops.!

"Come on, Rashmi. Let's start an intravenous line with ten percent dextrose. I will also inject the vitamin B-1 through the line."

Chandu checked Amir's pulse and breathing. His blood pressure was a little low, but his heart sounds were alright. He will live! After about five minutes, Amir slowly opened his eyes.

"Praise be to God," he said in Arabic. He took Chandu's hand and kissed it!!

After another half an hour he was having a nice conversation with Rashmi in Arabic. When he was stable enough to get up and walk, they said goodbye to Amir and headed back to the hospital.

"You know, Doctor, Amir thinks you definitely saved his life!

He was asking me what kind of drinks you prefer! I told him you like Johnny Walker Black Label scotch. I learned it from Dr. Manuk. So you can expect at least a few bottles of scotch from him!"

"Well, maybe some day he can do me a favor when I am ready to go back the the states!" Chandu laughed.

"That's true. He is very influential. If he clears you, you don't need anything else." She was very happy with the outcome.

Over the months, Chandu had a very cordial relationship with the nurses and the nursing director.

"Oh, by the way, we should be getting all the cardiac monitoring equipment from Japan tomorrow. I need your help in setting it all up and maybe we can impress some of our Sultans!" Chandu was very excited to upgrade the intensive care unit. He got back to bed and turned on the Akai tape recorder to listen to some of the music he had taped. It was very comforting.

Chapter Twenty

All the staff members had gathered around to watch the new monitoring system. There was a lot of excitement. It so happened that King Faisal's personal bodyguard had been just brought in by ambulance from Riyadh. He had suffered a stroke and was unstable. This was just perfect for Chandu to show his skills. He connected the monitor to Abdulla, the bodyguard, and was able to show everyone how they can see the actual heart-beats, breathing, etc. There was the administrator, Tarik Aziz, watching all this in awe, and he said, "We are so glad that we hired you, Dr. Chandu. I think we have the best intensive care unit now! Thank you for getting the most modern equipment. I am really impressed!"

"You are most welcome." Chandu was very humble. "Next thing we need is adding a CT scan unit to our radiology department. You should look into it, Mr. Aziz." Chandu was very busy looking at the monitor and trying to analyze the data. Abdulla's vitals were steady although his blood pressure was high. He asked the head nurse to give intravenous medication to lower the blood pressure. After he was stable, he performed a lumbar puncture to check the spinal fluid. This was blood tinged, indicating brain hemorrhage.

"This does not look too promising," he continued, "but we will continue to monitor. Let's give him one hundred milligrams of prednisolone through the IV line. This will reduce the brain swelling," he told the nurse. After abut two hours, Abdulla was responsive to commands. This was encouraging. During the night rounds there was much progress. Now Abdulla was able to talk to the nurses and was eager to find out what had happened to him.

The next morning, when Chandu went to make rounds in the intensive care unit there were some important visitors. They were sent by King Faisal to find out about his bodyguard's condition. The health minister shook Chandu's hand and said to him in good English, "Thank you very much, Doctor, for saving Abdulla's life. I see you have all the new monitoring system! That is really great. If there is anything else you need, please let us know and we will see to it that it's done. O.K.?"

"Thank you very much, Amir," Chandu replied. "I will let Mr. Aziz know if I think of something in the future."

The next day when he was in his room making coffee, a gentleman knocked on the door. Driver Ali was at the door. "Doctor Saab, you are invited to a dinner party at the health minister's house tonight."

Ali was on time. Chandu sat back and looked out the window from the back seat. The view was spectacular. Brilliant golden setting sun was reflecting over the clear blue waters of the gulf and the sand dunes were casting a shadow against the walls of several homes on the way.

"You will like Amir's place, Doctor," Ali said as he was playing with the car radio. "He has five wives and maybe fifteen childen," he laughed. Now he turned on a station that was playing popular belly dancing music.

When they approached the home of the Amir, Chandu saw something he never expected to see! It was more like a mini palace!! Built of Italian marble and looked like a mausoleum! "Wow! A little Taj Mahal!" he thought.

The security guards opened the gate to let the car in the compound. Two other uniformed guys escorted Chandu into the main hallway. Amir was waiting there with Tank Aziz, the administrator.

"Welcome doctor! Welcome to my humble place!" he said. Chandu took off his shoes as it was customary and put the linen booty over his socks. Amir, himself, was in his formal Saudi dress. Gold chains were obvious around his neck. He had diamond rings adorning four of five fingers on his left hand and a diamond laden Rolex watch around his wrist. He took Chandu through the hall into a formal dining area. The dinner was set up on a huge silver platter surrounded by lots of fruits. The seats were all made of soft silk and had hand sewn rich gold flowers. Everyone would sit around, Japanese style, on the cushions and eat family style. The main course was a lamb dish filled with lots of nuts, spices and rice. The meat was very tender and tasty. Long stemmed crystal glasses filled with expensive French champagne were served.

"Here is to good health, Doctor! We are so glad to have you here!" Amir said, toasting the glass. "I have asked Mr. Aziz to have your contract extended by two more years!! If you need to go back to the states for a visit, or to get married there, you can bring your bride back here! If you don't find anyone there, we can find you a nice girl!" He laughed aloud.

Mr. Aziz also joined in. "That's right, Dr. Chandu. We will also double your salary! What do you think?"

"Well, that is really nice of you, Amir! I will have to think about it. As you know, I have already applied for my green card and I have to go to the American embassy in Beirut, Lebanon next week."

Chandu could hear women's laughter in another room across. As it was the Saudi custom, the women were separated from men during dinner! When he glanced around the room across, he could see women in full burkha and veil. He could see the gold jewelry around their wrists shining brightly.

After the dinner, Amir shook Chandu's hand and handed him a small package, a jewelry box wrapped in bright shiny paper.

"This is something for you, Doctor. You have our gratitude! Thanks." He shook hands firmly and took Chandu to the front door.

"We will see you at the hospital tomorrow, Doctor," Mr. Aziz said as he said goodbye.

Chandu got in the car and opened the gift box he had received. There was a handsome Bulova Accutron gold watch!! He was really touched. "What a nice gesture!" he thought. "Now I have to make up my mind about the contract."

He had enjoyed working at the facility, and with all the staff. But there was no social life! It was more like working in a prison-like environment. Other than work and making tax free money, there was nothing exciting. It was very nice that he was able to send money regularly to India to help with his sister's wedding and his father's long time dream of building a small home.

After he got back to the room, he started writing a letter to Raj. They had been in touch on a regular basis. Any day now Raj would be a father. How exciting! By the time Chandu would get back to the states, he would become an uncle to Raj's son!! After he finished the letter, he started working on a case .presentation he was doing at the teaching hospital in Dahran. 'This was an interesting case of a British lady that had contracted an infectious disease called 'Brucellosis,' acquired through ingestion of contaminated goat milk! It had taken some clever detective questioning and follow through that he was able to solve the case! It was treatable with antibiotics, and the lady was cured. Everyone was quite impressed with the way the case was handled. This was very well received by all the attendings at the teaching hospital after he presented the case.

Chandu arrived in Beirut, Lebanon, and he had made arrangements to stay at Al-Hamra, a posh downtown hotel. This was close to the big famous Casino D'Lebon, a French style casino. Chandu liked to visit the casino and play the slot machines. He was really not a big gambler, rather timid and conservative! Most of the time, slots that took quarters attracted him. At least he could spend some time there. The place was very crowded. There were people from all regions and different countries. Lots of super rich Arabic-speaking gentlemen were gathered around the roulette table! Special rooms with wide tables set up for high stake gamblers could be seen.

Cocktail waitresses with skimpy dresses floated around the gambling hall attracting looks! Chandu enjoyed watching all this, sipping his scotch.

"You must be an American." Chandu spotted the guy sitting next to him.

"Yeah! I am touring the Middle East. I am from Chicago, Allen." He extended his hand and shook hands with a firm grip.

"I am Dr. Chandu. Just call me Chandu," he smiled and continued, "What do you do, Allen, in Chicago?"

"I run a software company. Where do you practice?"

Chandu explained his part of the story and said, "I am actually here to get my permanent visa, going back to the states."

"You should look into Chicago, a great place. Lots of good hospitals."

"Well, I have been to Chicago. I took a postgraduate course before I took my boards. I do like the city! But having lived in Buffalo, near Niagara Falls, N.Y., I kind of like a smaller city." Chandu was being sincere.

"I see your point," Allen agreed. "I guess it's all individual taste."

Chandu inserted a quarter into the slot machine and pulled the handle. A small jackpot!! He gathered the hundred quarters and said goodbye to Allen. He went to the cashier and collected his winnings and headed back to the hotel. On the way to the door, there were some pimps soliciting rich clients! Chandu nodded and walked away and got into the limo. The next day he had the appointment with the immigration office. After nearly two years, he can now begin to relax!

He also plans to visit a few countries before he would be back in America. Now he can afford to do this, thanks to Saudi Arabia!!

Chapter Twenty-One

"Hey, honey, I got a letter from Chandu today." Raj was very excited! "He is leaving Saudi Arabia in ten days. He got his permanent visa! How great is that! He will be back by the second week of next month!"

"That is such wonderful news. I know how much you have missed him," Lynette continued. "Do you think he will come back to Buffalo?"

"I am sure he will. Remember, his chief at the VA medical center had promised him a position as a staff member."

"I guess, now that you mention it." Lynette smiled. "Our baby will be two weeks old when he gets back! I just can't wait to hear all the stories and adventures of his travel."

Raj poured a glass of scotch and started sipping slowly, and pulled Lynette close to him and gently rubbed her belly! The baby seemed to react as well, and threw a punch! They both laughed. The telephone rang.

"Hi, Raj. Would you like to assist me in surgery tomorrow morning?" That was Dr. White, an orthopedic specialist.

"Sure, Adam. I have a ten o'clock case, a gallbladder. I hope yours is earlier!"

"Yeah, I start mine at 7:30 in the morning. So, I will see you at breakfast."

He hung up the phone. "Well, I guess we better get to bed early tonight, Hon." Raj kissed Lynette on her lips. He was prepared to work hard. Now there will be the baby! "I know I don't spend too much time with you. But I have to do this for us and the baby!" Raj was apologetic.

"I wish you could be with me all the time. But I know I am married to a surgeon! Just make sure you are around when I'm ready to have the baby. I need you in the delivery room, O.K.? Promise me!"

"Don't worry, Lynette. No matter what call comes in, I will be there for you!" Raj gave her a hug.

The T.V. was on. The news anchor was narrating a story about a drug bust in downtown. The next story was about the closing of Republic Steel in south Buffalo and more job losses. "Not good news," Raj thought. The weather report was not good as well.

They were predicting an early winter! "What else is new?" Raj remembered the days when Chandu and him walked in the snow on Jefferson Avenue near Sister's Hospital. That was then! Now he was getting a little sick of the cold and snow!! He was getting tired. He turned the TV off and headed upstairs. Lynette was already sound asleep! As he looked at her peaceful face, a strange sense of satisfaction flashed across his mind. He was ready to face yet another day.

Raj had to get out of bed early that morning. He had a long day in surgery. He was to assist the senior with his cases, and he had his own three cases scheduled. Lynette was still sleeping. He got up quietly and went down to the kitchen, made himself a strong cup of coffee and drank a glass of orange juice and thought he would grab something to eat in the hospital cafeteria before starting surgery. That was the usual routine for most of his mornings except on weekends, when he would have a chance to have breakfast at home with Lynette.

He arrived at the hospital staff room and was greeted by Dr. White. "I see you are here bright and early, Raj." He smiled.

"Yeah, I am assisting in total gastrectomy case with Dr. Barone this morning. I don't know where he finds these cases. Do you?"

"He has a big referral base from all the family does! Big parties at his house and all the expensive Christmas gifts will do it!" Dr. White was serious about this.

"Let's go have some breakfast." Raj headed to the elevator. They got down to the cafeteria and placed some scrambled eggs, sausages and a few pieces of bacon on a plate and sat at the table. There was the Buffalo newspaper. Raj pulled the sports pages out and started reading. The Buffalo Sabres were hiring a new coach and some new players were joining the team.

Raj heard the operator page his name. He answered the call. Lynette was at the other end. "Raj, Honey, my water just broke! I think I am going to have the baby soon!! Can you come home quick?"

"Lynette, calm down, slow down! I am at the hospital. Can you call our neighbor, Dorothy? If you can't get her just call 911 and I will meet you here. I am going to wait for your call." Raj sounded panicky.

"Your wife is having the baby! Wow! Raj, forget the cases this morning. Your wife needs you to be by her side. Other things can wait!" Dr. White was reassuring.

"I have to cancel all my cases, and I have to tell Dr. Barone that I won't be able to assist him this morning." Raj called the operator and had her page Dr. Barone.

He never expected the baby would decide to arrive this day!

Within minutes, Lynette was on the way to the hospital by ambulance. Raj rushed to the maternity floor and Lynette was already in the delivery suite being attended to by the nurses. Raj grabbed her hands and squeezed them gently. He bent down and kissed her forehead. Tears were rolling down Lynette's cheeks, and she was breathing hard. Dr. Jack Bartels showed up within a short time and greeted Lynette and Raj.

"So, you guys ready to do this? Remember the stuff you were taught in Lamaze classes. It's all in the breathing. O.K?" Jack was always easy going.

Raj moved behind Lynette's head and was ready to follow the Instructions!

"Push, Honey, push." The nurse encouraged Lynette! "There, there! I see dark hair! Here he is!! Raj, Junior! Wonderful!"

Jack was very happy. Raj and Lynette heard the new baby's cries and a shiver went up their spines!!

"This is for real!! Oh, my God. Our son is really here," Lynette sobbed.

"Congratulations. You two have a handsome boy! Do you have a name yet?" Jack asked.

"Yes, we do! Anoop! Anoop Raj, Junior." Raj was ecstatic.

"If all goes well, you will be home tomorrow!" Jack finished the necessary after treatment.

"You know, Hon, now that you already had the baby, let me go and make some money for the baby!" He continued, "I can go back and assist Dr. Barone and do my cases too.

Lynette was tired and was dosing off

"I will be back with you this afternoon! O.K.?" Raj didn't wait for an answer and left the delivery suite.

Chapter Twenty-Two

Raj started reading the letter he had just received from Chandu. "Dear Raj, first of all, let me congratulate you on the new addition to your family. Baby Anoop looks very much like his daddy! Well, I left Saudi Arabia two weeks ago and am enjoying my travels. The first stop was Hong Kong, and I was very much impressed by how advanced this place is. The city is very modern and full of life. I had an escort with me to give me a tour of the place. This one was a real professional young lady, and I really enjoyed having her around. We went to Tiger gardens and visited the village of Aberdeen. This is a nice fishing village on the waters and had a nice colorful floating garden. Kowloon shopping center was very nice as well. It had lots of electronic goods, cameras, you name it — they had it at discount prices! After three days stay there, I flew to Bangkok. Wow! What a place! It reminded me of India. All those scooters, bikes, streets jam packed with people from every corner of the world. I was staying at the Imperial Hotel, a very posh hotel with a five star rating. Lots of visitors stay there. I visited a couple of night clubs. Teenage prostitution is very big in Thailand. Anything for a dollar bill!!

You would have liked it! I am just kidding! Don't tell Lynette!! I visited the Golden Temple, nice architecture! After three days of stay, I flew to Tokyo, Japan! I was staying at the Intercontinental Hotel, closer to downtown. You would think you were back in New York!! Very much like Manhattan, Times Square and Broadway all over!! They have a beautiful subway system. I had a guide, a nice college kid who could speak English very well. He took me around the Imperial Palace. There were lots of young men and women. I enjoyed seeing a great Kabuki performance and enjoyed eating Japanese food and drinking saki!! I was thinking about you in all those places. Maybe some-day we can do this together!! I was really glad that I was able to do this now! As I crossed the International Date Line, while on Japan Air, I was given a certificate. Now that I have arrived back on the U.S. soil in Honolulu, I am thrilled to death!! I will be touring the eight islands here in Hawaii before I reach New York next week!! I can't wait to come and see you all back in Buffalo and catch up on the events. Kiss the baby for me and 'Hi' to Lynette. Bye for now, buddy! See you soon!" Chandu Raj had Lynette read the letter after he got home.

Chapter Twenty-Three

Air France airliner arrived on time at the J.F.K. airport. The skies were blue and the landing was perfect. Chandu's heart started pounding with excitement. After he approached the immigration officials, one took a look at his passport and said with a smile, "Welcome back, Doctor! Welcome back!!"

"Thanks very much Officer, good to be back!! Yes, indeed!!" Chandu replied. He went through the customs and said "I just have some souvenirs for friends, but nothing to declare otherwise."

" O.K., Doc, you are good to go!!" The officer was very cordial. Chandu got down to the baggage claim area and the place was very busy. He waited for his suitcase and looked for ground transportation.

On the way down, from a small gift shop he could hear the music playing. "Oh What A Feeling! Dancing On The Ceiling!!" by Lionel Richie!!

The song couldn't have been more appropriate, Chandu thought!

He was anxious to catch the next plane from LaGuardia airport to Buffalo, N.Y. He still had about two hours to spend at the airport.

"Hey, Raj! I am at the airport and will be leaving in two hours. I should be in Buffalo by eight o'clock. Can you pick me up at the airport?"

Raj was equally excited! "I will be there buddy! We will all be there!! Can't wait to see you after nearly five years!!"

Chandu's flight was on time.

"What will you have, sir?" the hostess was asking.

"Scotch and soda for me, thank you!" Chandu said while reaching for the packet of peanuts!

He sat back feeling completely relaxed as he took sips of good tasting scotch!! His mind was still on the predictions he had learned from Madame Francesca. As the plane touched down for landing, Chandu looked out the window and was very happy to see the familiar scenes around the airport! The buildings looked the same. Downtown skyline looked like it was five years ago.

As he walked towards the baggage area he could see hands waving in the air and someone shouting "Welcome back Chandu! Welcome back!!"

Raj was frantically waving his hands. Lynette was carrying baby Anoop! Chandu dropped his suitcase by his side and gave Raj a big bear hug!! Then he kissed Lynette and tried to pick the baby up! But the baby was shy and held on tightly to his mother!

Chandu and Raj stayed out late into the night sipping scotch and talking about everything that had gone on over the past five years! Since it was the weekend Raj didn't have to be at the hospital early.

"Hey, how are Nabha and Gopal? Are they still staying at our old place?" Chandu was curious.

"Yeah! They are still there. But I think pretty soon Nabha might be looking for a place for himself!!"

"Is that right? Why? Did they have a fight or what?" Chandu laughed.

"You know how Gopal is! Very stubborn! I guess Nabha has been bringing his girlfriend to the apartment and she does not care much for Gopal!! She can't take his jokes and his loud mouth!!"

"I know, I am surprised that they have lasted as long as they have! By the way, who is this girl friend?"

"A nice Irish nurse, she comes from a big family! The two get along very well! I think he is thinking marriage!!" Raj continued.

"Well, good for him!! How about Gopal? Does he have a steady girl friend?"

"You know him! He tries to go out with as many girls as he can! Tries to impress them! You know he is also specializing in surgery. He spends a lot of time at the race track!!"

"How about you? Do you still go to the track?"

"No, no! Are you kidding? Lynette will kill me! Now with the baby and all!!" "I bet you sneak out once in a while without telling her! Right?"

Raj just winked! "Shush!! She may be still awake!"

"All right buddy, let us get to bed. I will try to contact Dr.Augustine at the V.A. Medical Center Monday morning. Maybe tomorrow we will visit the boys!"

"That sounds like a plan. Maybe Gopal will cook his favorite, pork vindaloo!! Good night! If you need anything, you are at home! Help yourself! I have fresh towels in the guest bathroom. Maybe we can have breakfast at the Orchard Downs. Lynette will be busy with the baby! She doesn't mind if I hang out with you! Especially after five years!" Raj directed him to the guest room.

After an exhausting evening Chandu was ready for bed.

Chapter Twenty-Four

Chandu parked his car at the physician's parking lot of the V.A. Medical Center. He had an appointment to see Dr.Augustine, the chief of medical department.

As he went up to the eighth floor medical office he was greeted by Margaret, the secretary who had been there for more than twenty five years!

"Dr. Chandu, how good to see you back!" She greeted Chandu with a warm hug.

"Good to be back, Marge! Dr. Augustine around? He is supposed to meet with me."

"He will be right back. He has been expecting you! I am sure he will be happy that you are back!" As she was finishing, Dr. Augustine entered the office. "Dr.Chandu! You are back!! I think the timing is perfect!" He grabbed Chandu's hand and patted his shoulder.

"It so happens the attending physician who was in charge of the gastroenterology unit moved to Florida. We have an opening for a qualified specialist! I will recommend your name to the administrator. How would you feel?" Dr. Augustine continued, " I will take you to Andy, Chief of Staff! O.K.?"

Chandu was speechless! Things were happening fast!

"I can't thank you enough, Chief! What about the license?" He had not taken the NY State Board exam for licensure yet.

"No problem! You will have a temporary permit till you get your license."

" I really appreciate that, Dr. Augustine! I have to look for an apartment not too far from the hospital. I will start looking soon." Chandu was all smiles!

"O.K., let's go to Andy's office. I guess you will have to complete some paper work!"

Dr. Andrew was very cordial and he shook Chandu's hand and said, "Well, we are glad to have you back! I guess you can start next week. We really need an attending for 8-D ward. We have forty patients there, and two rotating residents are assigned to that floor. You will be in charge of making daily rounds, teaching, etc. You were the chief resident before! You already know all these! Right?" Dr.Andrew was very confident.

After a brief meeting Chandu had to go down to human resource office to complete all the paper work.

It was lunch time and he wanted to see if Dr. Atanacio was still working. "Hey! You are back!" Atanacio was very happy to see his old friend!

"So, you are a nephrologist now?" Chandu quizzed.

"Yeah, I did complete my internal medicine and went into nephrology. I am the guy if you need kidney dialysis for any of your patients! Keep that in mind!"

"Well, if I need any help with the routine here at the hospital, I will definitely call you!!" Chandu was sincere.

"Let's go have some lunch! How is the good old cafeteria? Still make good burgers and fries?" Chandu always liked their menu.

The two walked down to the cafeteria and everything looked the same! It seemed strange to be back there after five years and recognize some of the nurses!!

"Welcome back, Doctor!!" Chandu was very comfortable in his old place!

Chandu was happy to find a nice apartment with two bed rooms in Kenmore. This was about 15 minutes drive to the V.A. Medical Center and was near the shopping mall. Bud and Anita owned this apartment. A very nice couple from Grand Island. He retired as a captain of a coast guard boat and they had no children. They were very happy to have a physician as their tenant. The previous tenant had given them a tough time. She was single and had lots of teenagers hanging around. Loud music and lots of beer drinking! They had a hard time evicting her.

"Hey, Doc! We are so pleased you chose this place. If there is anything we can do to fix your apartment let us know." Bud was very sincere.

"I am very glad that I found this place, Bud! Close to the hospital and all the stores. Works out perfect for me. Hope you don't mind the smell of Indian curry once in a while! I love to cook." Chandu said laughing.

"Not at all! Maybe we like to taste your cooking! Only problem is my wife can't handle the hot food! You may have to fix her stomach!!"

"No problcm! I can handle that!" Chandu chuckled again!

After getting the keys to the place, Chandu called Raj.

"Hey, Raj! Guess what? I found an apartment in Kenmore. I will have to move from your place this weekend! Hope you can help me with the move. I can't thank you and Lynette enough for putting up with me!"

"What do you mean if I would help? Of course! What we can do, we can rent a U-Haul and we can do this in one trip!" Raj continued, "I guess we will see you tonight for dinner. We will order a large pizza with all the gorp from Santora's! How does that sound?"

"That's just great! Then we will have time to pack my stuff!! Not like I have a truck load or anything!!" Chandu laughed as he hung up the phone.

After Chandu got home, the pizza arrived as expected! The buddies sat in the backyard after pouring a couple of glasses of Miller Highlife beer.

Raj was somewhat silent. Perhaps he would see less of Chandu. "Make sure we get together on weekends, at least, buddy! Or I will kill you!!"

"You can't get rid of me that fast, boy! You guys have to come and eat at my new place! O.K.?" Chandu choked a bit!

They enjoyed the pizza. Baby Anoop was sleeping. Lynette stayed in the background leaving the two friends alone!

Chapter Twenty-Five

"Are you going to come home sooner today dear?" Lynette asked Raj who was getting ready to leave the house.

"Why, do we have something special?" Raj had no clue!

"Remember, we have to take Anoop to the doctors this evening. I made a late appointment so you can come with me. Is that alright?" Lynette was showing a little impatience.

"Hope I can make it on time. I have three big cases today and I have to assist Dr. White. He has four hip replacement surgeries! You know what to ask the doctor. You don't need me there if I can't make it!" Raj had already made up his mind that he would skip the doctor visit. He knew the pediatrician well and he would take good care of Anoop!

"O.K., Honey I am going to take off now!" he said as he planted a kiss on her lips.

Lynette was not too happy, but she had no choice being married to a surgeon. There were a lot of days she would be home alone with the baby. She looked forward to weekends when Raj had some more time at home. After he finished surgery he was tired and stiff. He heard a familiar voice!

"Hey , Raj! I have my horses running tonight at the Hamburg race track. You want to come?" That was Dr. Barone.

"You know, I was supposed to be home early to take my boy to the doctor with my wife. But I guess it is already late. I can stay for a few races with you." Raj needed to relax after a tough day.

He recalled surgical nurse, Brenda, saying to him during the middle of assisting, "You look very tense, Doctor Raj. I have not seen a smile on your face since you had your boy! I think you need some TLC," she teased him. Raj always liked Brenda. She was tall and buxom with curly dark hair.

She was in her early thirties and apparently single. She enjoyed outdoor activities, very friendly, obviously took care of her body very well!!

She enjoyed working with Raj and always admired his skills. She also knew that Raj was very attracted to her, just the way he would react in the operating room. Her heart pounded every time he came close to her and leaned against her body. Some of the other nurses had commented about their closeness.

"Maybe you should go out with him!" they would say.

"We know he is married and has a boy! So what? You are single and can have some fun!"

Brenda just kept her mouth shut and smiled.

It was not a very good day at the track for Raj. Dr. Barone's horses lost the race.

On the way home, Raj was just thinking of excuses for coming home late.

"I expected you to come home early today, Raj. What happened? Don't tell me you had another case to do!" Lynette had anger in her voice.

"Well, Dear, I told you about my case load. If I don't work I don't earn! Plain and simple!" Raj was curt and was trying to cope with his losses at the track!

"Anoop needs some blood work. Dr Arun, the pediatrician told me. You know why? Maybe you should ask your friend." Lynette was still sounding angry.

"I am going to see Arun tomorrow and I will ask him. I think it is just routine." Raj was trying to reassure her.

"Daddy! You are home!" Anoop jumped into Raj's arms! Raj hugged and kissed Anoop and there was instant calm. They both were busy playing with Anoop's trucks!

"You know it's already late. Why don't we order a pizza from Santora's and maybe some hot wings!!" Raj wanted to forget about the day's events.

After they had the dinner, Raj had scotch and soda and chased it with a beer! He held Lynette close and said "I am sorry,

Honey! I will do my best to spend as much time as possible with you and Anoop! But you know my line of work! Emergencies happen and I have to be ready. I chose this profession to help people. It gives me great satisfaction when I see a sick person get well after I take out a gallbladder or appendix!" He continued, "Also, we have to start saving for college for Anoop! It's never too soon!"

Lynette gently stroked Raj's face and kissed him passionately!

"I am going to take Anoop to bed and see you in a little bit." Lynette headed upstairs.

Raj went through his mail and decided to call Chandu. He had not seen him in almost four months. Chandu had been very busy as he had assumed attending's position at the V.A.Medical Center.

"Hey, this is your buddy! How the hell are you? I have not seen you in months." Raj missed his company.

"You guys are busy with the baby and your work! As you know, I am in charge of the GI service and I am responsible for teaching residents. That really keeps me busy. After I come back to my apartment I do the cooking and cleaning!! I can't afford maid's service! I am not a rich surgeon like you, boy!" Chandu was teasing with a laugh.

"How about this weekend? Why don't you come to our house for dinner? Maybe Lynette can make a nice chuck roast." Raj wanted to see Chandu.

"O.K., Raj, I will bring some champagne and snacks. Let's catch up!" Chandu was happy to hear from his friend.

Chapter Twenty-Six

"Hey! Come on in, buddy!" Raj greeted his friend with a hug.

"Here, I have some flowers for Lynette and a bottle of Great Western for you." Chandu handed them to Raj.

"Uncle Chandu! Uncle Chandu!" Anoop came and jumped on Chandu.

"I have something for you too! Here is a fire engine you would like." He handed Anoop the toy. Anoop grabbed the toy and left the room running.

"I can't believe how grown the boy is! He is looking more like you!" Chandu was absolutely right! Anoop was a mirror image of his daddy.

"You boys want to relax! I will pour the drinks! Thank you, Chandu, for the beautiful flowers! They are so colorful and pretty. I don't remember your buddy bringing home flowers!!" Lynette was teasing.

"I just brought you flowers the other day. For your birthday, remember?" Raj was serious.

"I know, I know! Can't you take a joke, Dear?" Lynette snapped back.

"All right, let's toast!" Chandu grabbed the champagne glass and clinked Raj's glass. Lynette went back to the kitchen to finish preparing the meal. The two friends went out to the back porch and sat down on the swing set.

"So, what is happening Raj? Is everything 0.K?" Chandu was curious.

"Well, you know how women are! Damned if you do! Damned if you don't!" Raj continued, "You know how hard I work. Surgery schedule is tight! Sometimes I get home late and I don't have the energy to spend time with Anoop! That ticks her off! What can I do?"

"You have to have lots of patience, buddy! The boy will never know his daddy. Try to spend as much time as you can, at least during weekends!" Chandu continued, "You can always say no, when they call you to assist in a case. You've got to have your priorities in line. I don't blame Lynette."

"I try my best, but that is not enough for her." Raj sighed.

"Hey, somebody told me that they saw you at the track! How do you sneak out without Lynette knowing?" Chandu was firm.

"I know, that is another problem. Lots of time I make up stories. Having to attend a meeting or emergency surgery, you know that kind of excuses!" Raj was honest with his friend.

"Another thing I want to tell you! Don't tell this to anyone! I have this beautiful nurse assistant that helps me in surgery, Brenda is her name! Oh boy, she really has a crush on me!! She is single and I am stuck!! What can I do?" Raj was hoping for advice.

"You must be out of your mind, boy! Don't even think!! You will be killed!" Chandu was emphatic.

"Are you boys hungry? Come in! Dinner is served!" Lynette shouted. The two looked at each other and quietly walked to the dinner table.

Chapter Twenty-Seven

It had been almost six months since Chandu started working at the V.A.Medical Center. His brother, Andy, was coming to Buffalo to obtain a master's degree in education. He had been a teacher in India. He had been accepted at Canisius College in Buffalo. He was thrilled that his older brother would be there to help him. At least he didn't have to pay for room and board! Besides Chandu had a helper at home in doing chores! After Andy arrived in Buffalo, Chandu had little time to visit Raj.

"Hey, Chandu! I think I have a big problem!" Raj sounded panicky.

"What's wrong, buddy? I know I have not seen you in months. You know my brother, Andy, is here with me now to get his master's degree. I have been very busy at the hospital. Tell me what is happening?" Chandu was very apologetic.

"Lynette has given me the ultimatum, boy. She has had it with me. My excuses for coming home late you know! I guess one of the lady's husband, one of our neighbors, saw me at the race track the day I was to baby sit Anoop. She had a garden club meeting to attend and asked me to be home that night. I tried to beg and plead. I told her I would forever stay out of the track!" Raj was now sobbing.

"Hey, calm down! Calm down now, Raj. I will tell you what, I am going to see both of you this weekend. I won't bring Andy with me. O.K.? Don't tell Lynette that I am coming. Just make sure she is home. Oh, and another thing. Can you have Anoop taken to his grandma's place? Then we can talk!" Chandu had a plan. He knew Lynette thought of Chandu as a family member and she also knew how much Anoop liked 'Uncle Chandu.'

"All right, buddy, I trust you completely. I am besides myself. I will make sure she is home and Anoop with grandma," Raj said with a sigh.

It was Saturday evening. The skies were gray and the humidity was unusually high that day. Chandu drove to Raj's Orchard Place home. He went to the door and rang the bell. Raj opened the door and Chandu could see that his buddy's face was swollen and dark circles under his eyes were glaring. There was loud music in the background. It was Roberta Flack's 'Killing Me SoftlyWith His Song.' Lynette was sitting on the couch next to the record player. Chandu could see her face all flushed and tears running down her cheeks. She just looked up at Chandu as he walked inside the house and shook her head.

"It is over, Chandu! It's over! Your buddy cheated me. I trusted him so much. I can't believe a single word he says! Every time we had to do something as a family, he is never there. He always has excuses! Surgery! Surgery! This meeting! That meeting! It is always an emergency! I've had it!!" She started crying loudly.

Chandu went down to her, held her close and said, "Lynette! Please listen! Don't do anything rash! Think of Anoop! You two have had a great life together. Think back to the days when you were dating! I think you two need to take a nice vacation. Maybe go on a cruise. Have you been able to talk to your pastor about the problem, Lynette?"

"We both talked it over with Father Joseph and he said the same thing you are telling now!" Lynette sounded very frustrated.

"You know, Chandu, it is really hopeless! You know what happens when we go on vacation? He always has some surgical book with him and he buries himself in it! We don't even talk to each other anymore. 'When was the last time you asked me how I feel about things dear?' Tell him!" Lynette snapped.

"I really try my best, Chandu, but, but!" Raj didn't finish!

"No buts! No ifs!! I have had it with you, Dear!" Lynette had already made up her mind.

"Chandu, you are a good man with a great heart! But we can't live like this! He is a surgeon and always will be! I need a husband and a father to my son! Not a part time one!! I am going to move with my mom next week!"

Chandu sat still for a few minutes and sadness overcame his emotions. "Lynette, please, I beg you! Please don't act on impulse. Give it some thought. Anoop needs a father. I know what Raj has done can't be undone. But you two can start fresh. I promise you two that I will do my best to keep my buddy in check. I also suggest that you two see a marriage counselor and get help." Chandu was fatherly in his advice!

"Chandu! I love you! But nothing is going to work! Our relationship is so broken, it is too late to fix it! My mom loves Raj and she is also distraught about what is happening!" Lynette held back her tears.

"All I can say is I am going to pray for you two! May God give you the strength to cope with the current situation. I still hope you two can work this out for everyone's sake." Chandu took a deep breath.

Raj looked totally helpless and he grabbed Chandu's hand and sobbed. "It is over! It's over! I brought this on myself! I will have to pay for it. Raj continued, "Chandu, thank you for all you have done for us! I know you are there for us when we need you! We will have to sit down and talk to Anoop! He is still too young to comprehend. I really don't know how he will react. I have to tell him you are going to stay with Mommy, and I will come and visit." Raj broke down and couldn't finish the sentence.

It started to rain outside! They could see the lightening flashes and hear the roaring thunder. It felt like God was shedding tears, as well. Chandu walked out after kissing Lynette and hugging Raj tightly.

Chapter Twenty-Eight

Mr.Cunningham, the attorney was very fair. Raj did not want to contest the divorce. "Irreconcilable differences" was the final verdict. Family Court Judge Arcata was also helpful. He granted joint custody of Anoop, and Raj had to pay alimony and child support. They would split summer vacation taking care of Anoop, and Raj would help with Anoop's future college expenses. Lynette was very cooperative and did not argue. She was allowed to take whatever she had before they got married and the rest they would split. She would get half of the equity of the home's current market value minus half of the balance on the mortgage.

Chandu was at the courthouse when the judge granted the divorce and it felt like the balloon had burst! He had tears in his eyes, and after the papers were signed, Raj walked over to Chandu and hugged him tight, visibly shaken and crying like a baby. Anoop was with his grandmother and both their thoughts turned to him.

"What just happened buddy," Raj sobbed.

"Hey, life will go on, Raj. You have to be strong and take care of that boy of yours. Now you may have to work harder. But everything will work out O.K.!" Chandu had to be encouraging.

"I will tell you what! Let's go to my place and get drunk! Andy won't be home. You can stay at my place till morning. I don't want you to drive tonight. O.K.?" Chandu grabbed his friend's shoulder.

"I have to see Anoop! How can I face him? What do I tell him? He is still very young, Chandu."

"Well, in some ways that is better. He won't understand what just happened. Someday you will be able to explain it to him," Chandu continued, "Let's go!" Chandu had driven Raj to the court house, since he was in no shape to drive. They got in the car and Chandu hit the expressway.

"You know, I thought I had everything going for me. Lynette, a beautiful girl that I loved and married, and a precious boy. What came over me! I lost it all, buddy! I am so stupid, damn stupid! I don't think I will ever get married again after this!" Raj was very apologetic for his actions.

"You have to get your act together, boy! I know you will. Forget the race track! I am sure there will come a time you will find happiness in life. You will find a life partner again! I am positive." Chandu was very sincere.

They got to the apartment and Bud, the owner, was just leaving after fixing a problem in the upstairs' apartment.

After they got in, Chandu pulled out a bottle of Johnny Walker's and poured two tall glasses with ice and handed one to Raj.

"Here's to the future! I pray God that you find happiness in life soon my friend." Chandu clicked his glass and took a long sip.

They sat in silence emptying the glass of scotch wondering what lay ahead .

Chapter Twenty-Nine

Gouramma could not believe what she was hearing. Raj's brother, Vikram, sat next to his mother and was reading the letter he had received from America.

"I am so sorry I have to let you know that I am now divorced. I am devastated and I have to look after my dear son, Anoop. I am very sorry that I disappointed you all and I brought this on myself. I don't blame Lynette."

Gouramma started to cry.

"I told him before he got married. Think very hard! You are marrying a girl that knows nothing about our culture. Nothing about our religion, nothing! But he went ahead anyway! Now look what happened! Who is going to take care of him? What's going to happen to my grandson, Anoop?" She kept on crying.

Vikram held her close and said, "Maybe this is all for good. I am going to ask him to come to India and maybe we can find him a new companion."

"I hope he can find happiness again. Only problem is who is going to marry someone divorced and has a kid to take care of? Oh, my God, why me? Why?" Gouramma slapped her head several times!

"Mother, please don't! Please don't! I know somebody in Bombay, and the parents are looking for a well settled foreign boy, especially a doctor! I am going to contact them tomorrow and I will call Raj to make arrangements to come home to India soon." Vikram was the caretaker ever since his father passed away a few years ago.

" I am going to light incense sticks and say a prayer! That's all I can do!!" Gouramma left the room.

Vikram started searching his phone book and after a few minutes was able to locate what he wanted.

This was a rich family in Bombay and they had a daughter who had finished law school and was looking for a law firm to join. By Indian standards she was well past the average wedding age for girls! The family was anxious to find a suitable bridegroom for her. This girl was very bright and also apparently a good cook. She had seen some boys that the parents had selected for her but none of them made an impression on her!

She always wanted to marry someone trained and working in England or America.

"Hello, this is Vikram here! I am calling from Bangalore. Is this Mr. Bhupathi?" "Yes! This is he!! Who is calling?" Bhupathis's voice was strong!!

"Vikram! I am Gouramma's older son! We live in Shankarapuram! I guess you are a distant cousin of my mother!!"

"Oh, yes! Gouramma was married to Biddappa who was related to my uncle! What can I do for you, Vikram?" Bhupathi was polite.

"You know my brother, Raj? The surgeon who went to America few years ago?" Vikram continued, "He is single now! He was married to an American girl but that didn't work out. He is divorced. He is now in Buffalo, N.Y. and he has a great private practice. A very good surgeon. We thought your daughter might be suitable for him!!"

"We will be very interested to pursue this, Vikram! I am going to have a talk with my daughter, Malathi, and let's see what she thinks! You know, nowadays you have to go by what they think and say!! Not like our old days! If our parents asked us to do something, we did it with no questions asked! Right?" Bhupathi knew his daughter very well!! "Oh, by the way is your brother coming to India any time soon?"

"I am going to be talking to him and I can find out when he can take some time off from work." Vikram was encouraged by the conversation.

"I would like you to give me a recent photograph of Malathi, if you don't mind! I would like to send that to my brother. I have his picture and you can show that to Malathi!" Vikram knew how to proceed in these matters!

"O.K.! We will look forward to hearing from you again, Mr.Bhupathi. Thank you very much! If God's willing everything should be smooth! Bye for now." Vikram hung up the phone.

Gouramma was very pleased to hear the details from Vikram. Maybe the prayers were being answered after all!!

"Make sure you call Raj and tell him to make arrangements to come to India. The sooner the better! Girls can change their mind quickly!" Gouramma was still worried that Malathi might reject a divorcee, especially one with a three year old boy.

Malathi came home from work and was sipping a cup of tea when her father came and sat next to her.

"Hey, Malathi, we have some good news for you! Gouramma's son called me today, and I guess his brother in America is now single. He is a great surgeon and does make a lot of money! I know you are looking forward to going overseas. You have had no luck in finding the right one so far! This is his picture! Look, he is very handsome, fair and tall!! Take a look!!" Bhupathi was looking at his daughter's face for a positive reaction!

"Daddy! You say that about everybody!! I think you want to get rid of me!!" Malathi was teasing. She held the picture in her hand and looked at it for a few minutes. Her thoughts shifted to a glamorous life in America! Marrying a surgeon!! That can't be true. A smile flashed across her face and a faint blush was noticeable.

"So, what do you think? You guys can exchange thoughts by mail till he comes to India, probably next month." Bhuapathi had positive thoughts.

"You know, Daddy, I want to take advanced courses in law also. I hope he will be supportive. He was married to an American girl! I am not sure how he will get along with an Indian girl!" Malathi was serious.

"Well, God will guide us with the decision. Let's wait for his visit." Bhupathi gently patted his daughter's shoulder and smiled.

Chapter Thirty

"Hey! This is Raj. I have some news for you. I will be going to India next month." Chandu was curious. He had not talked to Raj in two weeks.

"How are you doing, boy? Now that you are single, I hope you are not spending too much time at the race track!! Are you? What's happening in India?"

"Well, there is a distant cousin of my mother in Bombay. He has a daughter who is practicing law and they want to marry her off!! I guess my brother had a talk with her father and the girl is interested in coming to America!! My brother sent me her picture! She is kind of cute looking!! But I really have to meet her in person before I do anything!! So, what do you think?" Raj waited for advice.

"American girl didn't work out! If you really like this girl and your family has checked her out, maybe things might work out!! I think you should give it a shot, buddy boy!! Besides you need a mother at home for taking care of Anoop."

"I am not sure if they have told the other family about Anoop!! I will have to explain all that to her when I get to meet her." Raj had obvious anxiety.

"First get to know her, and then you can tell her about your divorce orders. It is not like you have full custody of Anoop. She only has to see the boy half the time, right?" Chandu was encouraging.

"I know that. But I will have to be very careful about mentioning my ex!!"

"I am sure she will quiz you about the American girl!! Best is to kind of gloss over and ignore the questions. You should tell her that the whole thing was a bad dream and you have nothing to do with her anymore!!"

Raj liked the advice he was getting from his close friend!

"I will tell you what! I will call you from India if anything develops. O.K.?"

"That will be fine. Just be careful mentioning anything about your earnings, etc.! You don't want her to be marrying you for the sake of money!! That would be very bad!! Remember that! I know you told me she comes from an affluent family. Who knows if she has expensive habits!! Kind of look around, and also try to ask her about her ambitions, likes and dislikes, etc. Also the most important thing is, if she likes kids!!" Chandu was impressive!

"O.K., Chandu! Thank you for all your advice. Too bad you can't come with me this time! But I expect you to be my best man if I decide she is the right one this time!! Wish me luck, buddy, and say a special prayer for me!"

"Don't worry, Raj, I certainly will be thinking of you and I will wait for your call." Chandu hung up the phone and looked up and took a deep breath.

Chapter Thirty-One

Raj was mentally and physically exhausted and he was anxious to see his family in India after nearly seven years. He was thinking of the day Chandu and he left India, and watching the teary eyes of all the family members saying goodby. This time it is different. He did not know what to expect. How was he going to face his mother? He had let them down real bad in his mind.

The aircraft landed safely at the Bangalore airport. After he cleared with customs he picked up his baggage and headed toward arrivals area where people were lined up to greet their family members and friends.

Raj noticed his brother, Vikram, waving.

"Hey, Raj! Glad you are back. I made Mother stay home. She has been very emotional and upset. She has been crying for days. She wants to see you!" Vikram hugged his brother with tears in his eyes. Raj fought back the tears as well.

"How is Mom doing otherwise? How is she health wise," Raj wanted to know.

"Her health is fine! But she can't wait to see you! She is hoping you will agree to many this girl, Malathi, after you two meet!" Vikram continued, "I think Mr.Bhupathi and his daughter will arrive from Bombay tomorrow. They should be at our house by late afternoon I think."

"That's good! That gives me some time to rest!" Raj smiled.

When they arrived home, Gouramma was waiting outside near the front gate.

"Oh! My God!! What ever happened to you? You are looking like a toothpick. Don't they ever feed you in America, son?" She gave a hug and stroked Raj's face.

"No, Mother! I have not lost weight! I am just tired! I didn't get much sleep on the plane." Raj was not very convincing!

"You are going to eat all your favorite dishes!! I have made bisibele bath and also curd rice for you! I have prepared some sweets also! We are going to fatten you up a little!!" Gouramma was not kidding!

"Mom, I can't eat all that rice dishes as I used to! But, certainly, I miss your cooking. My friend, Chandu, always reminds me what a good cook you are!!" Raj was thinking of Chandu.

"How is your buddy? If you are going to get married, I hope he will come for the wedding." Gouramma knew the two friends were inseparable. "Why don't you go take a shower and say your prayers while I finish cooking! O.K.?"

"All Right! Hope there is enough hot water for a nice bath! I hear you have problems with losing electricity and also water department tuning off water for hours!! Is that right?" Raj had heard this before.

"For the time being we are O.K. We got both just in time for you!!"

"Thank God! Here, Vikram, you take this suitcase upstairs. I have some goodies for you guys. I will unpack!"

Raj handed a bottle of Johnny Walker Black label to Vikram and winked! Vikram grabbed the bottle and hid that from his mother's view!

Gouramma was ready to impress the guests with her culinary skills! She was, after all, a great cook! She was going to prepare at least two sweets, two snacks and some spicy treats. These included Badam milk (almond milk), jalebi, a sweet pretzel like snack in syrup, masala vade (chickpea fritter), chakkali, a salty snack. She also prepared vanghi bath (spicy rice dish with eggplant) and kesar bath (saffron sweet rice). Raj was very impressed with his mother's menu selection.

"So, what time are they coming, Vikram?" Raj was getting a little anxious.

"They should be here in about two hours! Why don't you go get a hair cut and dress up for your new bride!" Vikram laughed.

"Well! She is not my bride yet! I haven't seen her, for one thing! Maybe I will go see my old barber! Is Nanjappa still there?" Raj enquired.

"Yeah! He is still alive and cuts hair even at his ripe old age of 75!! He can see well!!" Vikram replied.

"O.K. then! I am off to see him and will be back to have my face fixed!!" Raj got on his old bike and headed to the barber shop that was not too far from home.

"Hey! Doc!! Good to see you again. I hear you are going to have an . interview with a nice young lady! Is that true?" Nothing got by Nanjappa! If you needed to know what was happening in the neighborhood he would be the one with answers!!

"How did you even know?" Raj laughed and shook his hand. "Nanjappa, don't cut my hair too short! At least I want to keep the hair I have!! O.K.?" Nanjappa joined the laughter and proceeded to trim Raj's hair.

"I hear the American girls are very tough to live with! Is that so?" He was curious about what happened to Raj and his Ameican wife!

"That's is a long story, Nanjappa! They could be very sweet and at the same time they can squeeze everything out of you! You know what I mean? They can make you bankrupt, as they say, they can take you to the cleaners!! Now I have to start all overagain!" Raj felt better, like he was talking to his uncle!!

"Don't worry, Doc! Good things will follow! You are a good man!! So, how does this look?" He held a mirror to the back of Raj's head.

"This is great! Thanks very much. I will let you know what happens." Raj handed him a five dollar bill and left the place satisfied.

Chapter Thirty-Two

After the shower, Raj put on a nice silk shirt and wore blue corduroy slacks. He had a small mustache but no goatee! He splashed British Sterling cologne on his face! He looked in the mirror and winked at himself!!

He came down whistling softly as Vikram and Gouramma watched him with pride.

"You look very handsome, son!" Gouramma stroked his face and cracked her knuckles!! That is supposed to take away any bad luck!!

"I hope you are ready to meet Malathi!! Just don't scare her off!!" Vikram advised his younger bother. " Don't act like a surgeon! Don't ask too many questions!"

"I know! I know!! I can handle this, if you guys leave me alone. I am not a kid any more!" Raj was slightly irritated but quickly controlled his emotions.

The Ambassador car arrived near the gate. The driver got out and held the door for the passengers. Malathi got out of the back seat of the car. Her long dark hair was nicely braided and she had jasmine flowers covering her hair.

She wore a champagne colored sari with hand crafted gold designs! She had long diamond earrings and a pearl necklace with a solid gold coin in the middle with an etching of God, Srinivas. Her face was smooth as silk and she had gold colored sandals!! Her eyes were bright and dark. Mr. Bhupathi was a tall man in his late fifties. He had a dark Nehru jacket with matching pants on. He had a gift bag in his hand when they waked into the house.

"Welcome, Mr. Bhupathi, come on in! I am Vikram and this is my mother, Gouramma, you remember!" Vikram was very polite.

"Of course I remember you, Gouramma! This is my daughter, Malathi. I think you may have seen her when she was four years old!! She has grown since then!" He patted his daughter's shoulder.

"I see! She has really grown! She is beautiful. I don't think the picture says it all!! She is much prettier in person!!" Gouramma was sincere. Malathi blushed and smiled. Her eyes were wandering to see if Raj was around.

"Hey! Raj! Come down! We have company!" shouted Gouramma.

"I am right here, Mother!" Raj came down and shook Mr.Bhupathi's hand. Then he glanced at Malathi and suddenly a cold shiver went through his body!

"Hi! I am Raj! I had seen you long time ago when you visited here. Maybe we can go outside and get acquainted If that's O.K. with you, Mr.Bhupathi." He waited for the nod.

"Why don't you wait till they have some food first?" Gouramma wanted the guests fed first!

"This is something for you, Gouramma! For good luck!" Mr.Bhupathi handed her the fruit basket that was in the gift bag.

"Thank you! You shouldn't have taken the trouble! Let's eat!!"

They all enjoyed Gouramma's delicious menu. After they finished, Mr. Bhupathi suggested that Raj spend time alone with Malathi to get to know her.

"Why don't you two sit out on the front porch and have a chat!"

Raj opened the door and held it for Malathi with a big smile.

They sat out on the swing hung on the front porch. Raj could smell the sweet aroma of the fresh jasmine flowers of Malathi sitting next to her!

"So, what do you think of me Malathi? Does it bother you that I was once married?" Raj broke the ice after a few minutes of silence.

"Well! Yes and no!" Malathi answered like an attorney! She continued, "I am a little worried about your relationship with your ex wife!"

"There is no need to worry! That's all behind me now! Only time I might see her is when she brings my boy. We have joint custody and we have to share time with him. Vacation, etc. I love my son. I want to take care of him no matter what! I wish I had full custody, but our New York State law does not allow that unless I can prove that the mother was unfit or unstable!" Raj sighed and slightly choked with emotion thinking of Anoop.

"I understand that, Raj. But someday I want to have kids. I don't want my kids, our kids, treated differently. You know what I mean?" Malathi made her point.

"I promise you that I will take care our kids well and treat them all same. Just because Anoop's mother is American, he does not get special attention." Raj was emphatic, "I really mean this. If you ever decide to marry me, I will do my best to take care of you and the family."

"Raj! I have to confess! When I first got the news about you, I was very skeptical even thinking of marrying a divorced man! With a kid!! But my father has talked to me about you a lot. I know you are a great surgeon and the divorce was not your fault. When I was at the temple two days ago the priest blessed me and said my wishes would come true!! A rose flower dropped from God's right hand!! I guess that is a good sign!! I do want to come to America and maybe I can study as well. What do you think of me?" Malathi teasingly looked at Raj with sparkly eyes.

Raj looked at her up close and gently squeezed her hand and said, "You know the very first time I saw you, in my heart I knew you were the right choice.I will gladly take your hand! Would you be my wife?" Raj had noticeable tears on his cheeks.

"Of course I will and I will promise that I will take care of you and Anoop." She came closer to Raj and gently gave a quick hug.

The door opened and Mr.Bhupathi and Gouramma came out.

"How are you two getting along?" Gouramma could already sense relief!

Chapter Thirty-Three

"So, how did it go, Raj?" Chandu was curious as to what happened in India.

"You better get ready to be my best man buddy!" I think the wedding is going to be in Bombay. Let's start making arrangements for our travel!" Raj was excited.

"What dates are we talking about? Hope it's not next month! I have to go to Montreal for my fellowship ceremony!!" Chandu would never miss his friend's wedding.

"No, not next month! They need time to prepare, etc. It is going to be in August! August 12th Saturday! You know Malathi's father is quite well known and he has a huge number of friends and family members! It's going to be a big deal!!" Raj was not particularly thrilled since this was the second time around for him!

"How did Malathi react when you told her about Anoop?" Chandu asked.

"She was actually fine! Only thing she told me was that when we have more kids, they should all be treated equally!! Of course they would be!!" Raj had slight anger in his voice.

"That is to be expected, boy! You were married to an American girl!!" Chandu continued, "I am sure she will always be a little jealous of Anoop!!"

"That is true! Other thing I noticed, Malathi has expensive taste!! I could tell by her clothing and her jewelry!! I hope she doesn't get carried away!!" Raj was thinking.

"You have to be careful, buddy! You have to pay lots of attention to her and spend more time with her till you get to know her. It's not like you have known her for a year or two." Chandu's advice was right on cue.

"Pray for me, Chandu! Hope God will make this marriage last. I don't want to go through another divorce! Ever again!!" Raj sighed.

"Don't worry, Raj, I am going to give you all the moral support you need." Chandu continued, "Let's go the travel agency this weekend and make our travel arrangements. O.K.?"

"That will be fine! I have only half a day at the hospital Saturday. We can go there at three in the afternoon. You can come to my place and maybe later we can go for some chicken wings at Rooties!! That sounded good to Chandu. "I will see you around two-ish! You think you will be home by then?"

"Yeah! I will be home for sure. See you then! Bye for now!" Raj hung up the phone.

Chapter Thirty-Four

Chandu and Raj boarded the plane and arrived at JFK airport. Their flight to Bangalore was at eleven o'clock at night. Since they had a few hours to kill they decided to check the baggage at the airport locker and took a shuttle bus to downtown Manhattan. They stopped at a Brew Pub in Times Square.

It was a nice afternoon and sitting on the second floor, the sight was great. Beautiful tall sky scrapers with shiny glass windows and big bold signs on the buildings! The sounds on the street below, massive humanity of all colors, shapes and fancy outfits! The traffic was furious with yellow cabs and tour buses filled with tourists.

"What are you thinking, boy?" Chandu asked Raj who was quietly sipping a bottle of Heineken beer.

"I am a little scared about getting remarried, you know. Especially to an Indian girl. I know I had gone out with girls when we were in medical School! But this is a long term commitment!"

"You will do just fine, Raj. I am sure you have learned a thing or two from your failed marriage! You have to give her time and make her feel comfortable! You have to teach her American ways of life, and being an attorney, I am sure she should pick up on things quick!"

"I just hope so, my friend. I am also worried about how she will react when she sees Anoop, and of course my ex if she ever sees her!!"

"Time will tell! Don't worry about that now!" Chandu reassured. "Let's get something to eat before we head back to the airport. I like the Jamaican jerk chicken sandwich! How about you?"

"Yeah! That sounds good and goes well with the beer!!"

They were back at the airport with plenty of time to spare! Singapore Airline's jumbo jet had a full flight. They always liked the tremendous service, not to mention the very attractive flight attendants, young, charming and very friendly!

The plane raced towards the sky and down below they could see New York's million glittering lights and hundreds of shiny neon signs on buildings and billboards.

A pretty blonde flight attendant handed a couple of packets of peanuts and a napkin and asked in a sexy soft voice, "What will you gentlemen like to drink?"

"Johnny Walker Black label, please," Raj said!

"Same for me too," Chandu echoed! They sat back and plugged in the headset and started looking at the T.V. in front, above their seats.

Chapter Thirty-Five

Gouramma was very happy to see Chandu. "I am so glad that you could make it your friend's wedding! It wouldn't have been the same without you!! I know you are always there for him and that makes me feel better! Come in and have some of your favorite snacks!!"

"I would never miss your son's wedding or you great cooking!!" Chandu meant what he said.

"So, are we expecting a large gathering, Mother ?" Raj was curious. He would rather have a quiet private wedding ceremony if it were up to him.

"We are expecting two hundred people! Mostly friends of Bhupathi and his family. They can afford to spend big money! I tried to discourage him but he wants to have his daughter's wedding to be a memorable one. After all she is the only daughter and besides she is an attorney!!" Gouramma explained the situation.

"I guess you are right! This maybe Raj's second marriage, but for Malathi this is a big deal! Marrying a surgeon and living in America!" Chandu added his thoughts.

The wedding hall was very well decorated with lots of colorful ribbons and balloons! Gold and silver banners decorated the walls. The center stage was like a big carriage, the wheels were all covered with bright flowers and lots of costume jewelry with shiny crystals. One could see in the background colorful saris with gold and silver linings hanging as curtains. There was a band playing classical south Indian drums and instrumental music.

Raj was dressed in traditional Indian Dhoti, a wraparound dress, and a silk scarf around his neck. Malathi wore a bright golden bridal sari with rich red patterns showing along the edges. She had a diamond necklace, earrings and a small diamond nose ring. Gold bangles adorned her wrists and she had very colorful delicate paintings on the palms of her hands! She looked very happy as a bride!

"Well, just looking at her. I am sure she has very expensive taste," Chandu thought, but he would say nothing to Raj.

The two priests were very busy with the ceremonial fire, and their chanting echoed in the hall. The smoke was getting to Raj and he tried to avoid the draft. There was walking around the fire with the couple holding hands. There was also exchanging of flower garlands. The music got loud along with the chanting, and Raj tied a wedding necklace around Malathi's neck.

Then the couple bowed to the priests and then turned to Gouramma and Bhupathi.

Gouramma blessed the couple holding her hand over their heads and tears ran down her cheeks.

Chapter Thirty-Six

Raj came home from the hospital after a long day. His mind was still wandering around the wedding ceremony and a brief night he spent with Malathi after the wedding. He still felt awkward touching her and kissing her. He kept thinking of Lynette, the very first time they made love. He pulled into the garage and then walked to the mail box .

"Congratulations, Doc!" That was his neighbor, Dave. "When is your new wife coming from India?"

"Oh! Hi! Dave! She has to wait for her Visa. Hopefully soon! I am expecting her call any day now."

"Take care, Doc! See you later. If you need anything, please call me. O.K.?"

"Thank you very much. See you later, Dave." Raj stepped into the empty home. After changing his clothes he went to the bar and poured himself a shot of scotch with a splash of club soda and a couple of ice cubes. The drink felt good.
As he started to turn on the T.V. the telephone rang.

"Hello this is Malathi calling from India. Raj! Raj! Can you hear me?" For a split second Raj's heartbeat skipped!

"Hey! Malathi! I have been waiting to hear from you. So, what's happening?"

"I got my Visa!! I will be leaving Bombay this Friday and I should be in Buffalo Sunday afternoon!! I am excited, Raj! I missed you very much."

"I did too, Honey! You will really like it here. I can't wait to show you my home!! I should say our home," he corrected himself quickly!

"As soon as I get to New York I will call you from the airport. O.K.?"

"That's great. Too bad I can't come to New York. I have lots of patients at the hospital and I have to make rounds. I will be waiting for you at the airport here in Buffalo. I am going to call Chandu and I am sure he would want to greet you also."

"Do you need anything from here Raj? Your mother has given me some snacks, curry powder and few gifts."

"That's fine. I don't need anything. Just you, girl!! Take care. Travel safe." Raj blew a kiss and hung up the phone.

"Hey! Chandu! What the hell are you doing? Sleeping already?"

"Sleeping? Are you crazy! I just got home half an hour ago from the emergency room! I had to scope a guy with a piece of meat stuck in his esophagus!! I was able to pull it out!! This jerk was drinking and forgot to chew the meat!!"

"Hey! I just want to tell you Malathi will be coming Sunday! You want to come with me to the airport?"

"Of course I will!! Pick me up! Call me before you come. O.K.?"

Chapter Thirty-Seven

Malathi looked very tired from the long journey. She gave a quick hug and a soft kiss and Raj held her close for a few minutes and kissed her on her cheeks.

"You know my buddy, Chandu! He was my best man at the wedding, remember?"

"Yes! I do! How can I forget, that is your brother! Like your mom says!!" Malathi shook Chandu's hand and smiled broadly!

"O.K.! Now you are in America! Are you ready to spend the rest of your life here?" Raj was teasing.

"Now that I am here, I have no choice! Do I, Chandu?"

"I guess not! You must be very exhausted and hungry. Did they feed you on the plane?"

"I really did not care for their food! Everything is dry and no taste! The vegetarian dinner was lousy. I would rather cook at home!!" Malathi was also a good cook although not quite like Raj's mother! Since she was raised in Bombay she had picked up more northern style of cooking. She had learned to prepare some South Indian dishes from Gouramma.

The red Buick convertible that Raj enjoyed driving was racing towards Orchard Place.

"Here we are! This is our palace, Malathi! Now you are the queen here!!" Raj laughed as he pulled into he garage.

Malathi was struck by the size of the house and the big backyard surrounded by tall trees and woods and a small stream behind the property.

The house was quite spacious with a large living room, modern kitchen, four bed rooms upstairs including a master bathroom that had a shower and a Jacuzzi. The fixtures were all gold colored and marble top counters were shiny!

Raj had bought additional furniture after he came back from India. The place still needed a woman's touch. Some of the good furniture had been taken away by Lynette after the divorce.

"Well why don't you go up and freshen up. You probably want a nice long bath!" Raj guided her up the stairway.

Chandu made himself comfortable on the couch after pouring a glass of scotch and soda. He made one for Raj also and waited for him to come down.

"So, how do you feel now that your wife is here?" Chandu clinked his glass with Raj's and winked with a smile.

"I am a happy man! Hope my luck will turn for the better!! Now I have to plan for the honeymoon!! Let me know if you have any ideas!!"

They could here the sound of the shower upstairs.

The two friends sat there in silence slowly sipping scotch.

Chapter Thirty-Eight

Saturday afternoon Raj decided to take Malathi to Niagara Falls. Although he had seen the falls several times whenever anybody from out of town came to visit, that was the best known attraction. He knew Malathi would be very excited after hearing so much about the falls, one of the great wonders of the world!

"You know, it is so close to Buffalo but you will be surprised how many from here have not gone to see this wonder, Honey!" Raj was excited to show this marvel of nature.

"I am dying to see this too! I hear it is called the honeymoon capital! Is that right?" Malathi had done some home work!

"It sure is! Maybe we will stay over there tonight and have a real nice dinner at John's Flaming Hearth restaurant! You do eat meat, right?" Raj smiled.

"Of course I do! In Bombay you kind of get used to all kinds of food!!"

"That is good. When we came to this country, I could never eat beef! It tasted like shoe leather, if you know what I mean!" He continued, "The very first thing we liked was pizza, with lots of hot peppers!"

"I don't know if I ever had pizza in Bombay! But I have heard of it!" "Well, maybe we can have good pizza from Bocci's next week."

Raj pulled into the parking lot near the American Falls. The place was crowded. People from all over the world speaking in different languages were walking, holding hands, kissing and hugging!

There were Chinese, Japanese, Indian, French, Italian, English; they were all there!! Everyone with cameras and camcorders in hand, posing and clicking!! The flower trees were in full bloom and the green grass was lush.

Malathi was speechless as soon as she saw the giant waterfall. The thunderous sounds with splash of enormous cloud of water spray rising high and rolling back onto the huge rocks at the bottom of the falls was spectacular.

"Honey, you can really get close to the falls if we take that boat ride. You see all those people in funny blue and red plastic gowns?" We will take that ride. It is called the Maid Of The Mist! You will enjoy this!" Raj headed towards the boarding area. They picked up the protective rain gear with a hood! Raj helped Malathi with the plastic gown. They got up on the top deck to get a great view of the falls up close. The boat was jam packed with old and the young and lots of screaming children!

The captain of the boat greeted everyone and started a narrative tape giving the details about the Falls! As the boat got closer to the Horseshoe Falls, the excitement was building. The mist from the giant spray covered the gowns, and the children were clinging on to their parents, tight!!

Raj pulled Malathi closer and kissed her on her lips.

"I have never seen anything like this, Raj! This is awesome!! I am so glad that you brought me here, Honey! I know I like this place!!"

Chapter Thirty-Nine

"Hi! Honey! I got a call from Lynette and she is going to drop off Anoop. He is off from school on spring break and it is my turn to take care of him." Raj waited for Malathi's response.

"That is your son! Just don't ask me to meet your ex!! I don't want anything to do with her! I don't even want to see her!!" Malathi made it very clear.

"You don't have to see her! Besides she won't come into the house! If I see her car at the driveway I will go and pick him up!!"

Late afternoon Lynette's car was at the driveway and Raj went to get Anoop. Malathi was behind the window curtain and peeked through to get a glimpse of Lynette. She was curious about Raj's ex!!

Lynette got out of the car and took out a camping bag and a small suitcase from the trunk and handed them to Raj. Malathi wanted to see if there would be any physical contact between them! There was none, just a brief conversation as to when she would be back to pick him up. For one short moment, Malathi felt very jealous looking at Lynette. She could notice how attractive she was with her beautiful blonde hair and an ivory smooth complexion. What impressed her most was Anoop's startling resemblance to Raj. He was almost a spitting image of his father.

A very handsome boy! As the door opened she quickly moved out from her hiding and came to the door.

"This is Anoop, Honey! Anoop, this is Malathi. She is like your new mom!"

"Hello, Anoop! Glad to see you. You must be hungry. Come in, I have made macaroni and cheese. Hope you like it. Your daddy said you like that, and also peanut butter and jelly sandwiches. Is that right?"

Anoop just nodded and held on to his father!

"O.K., buddy! Let me take you to your room. Do you have any home work?" Raj carried the camping bag and the suitcase upstairs.

"Honey I have asked our neighbor, Dr.Sabharwal and his wife, to come for drinks. I think you met them very briefly the other day."

"Maybe I should make some snacks to go with the drinks. I hear they come from a very rich Gujarathi family in Bombay." Malathi was anxious to make friends with Mangala, the doctor's wife.

"That sounds good. Can you make some pakoras? Make it spicy! They like it that way. I think we have some coriander chutney to go with it!!"

"We have some eggplants, onions and potatoes. I can make pakoras using those. I can make some masala tea also for Mangala! You boys get ready." Malathi headed to the kitchen.

"Come on in Sab! How are things going for you, Doc? And how are you Mangala?"

"We are doing great, Raj! We are pleased to meet Malathi. As you know our family also comes from Bombay!" Mangala shook Malathi's hand.

"Pleased to meet you too. I understand my dad and your dad know each other very well. Is that right?" Malathi was very happy to meet someone close to her family.

"That's correct. Mr. Bhupathi and my dad both worked for the Reserve Bank Of India." Malathi brought a big tray of snacks and Raj poured the drinks.

"I will have a glass of white wine," Mangala said.

"Scotch for me as usual, Raj." Sabharwal laughed.

"Cheers!! Here is to your health and wealth!!" They clinked their glasses.

"You know I don't think I have been here since your divorce, Raj!" Mangala said.

"I think we ladies will go in the kitchen and get to know each other. You boys can sit here or in the backyard. Let us know if you need more pakoras!!"

Mangala was anxious to get to know more about Malathi. She had heard from her family about Malathi's expensive tastes in clothing and jewelry, etc. Malathi already had noticed Mangala's big diamond ring and her sparkly red ruby necklace and her pearl and gold bangles. Diamond earrings matched her necklace.

"It must be very hard for you, Malathi. Poor Raj has lost half of his good stuff! His ex-wife practically cleaned him out! Now the boy needs to be taken care of, as well. What do you think?" Mangala looked at Malathi .

"It is not easy, Mangala. I have to get used to this life. I don't know if you are aware that I was practicing law before the marriage!!"

"Yes, we found out about that. Do you think you will continue that profession here?"

"Well, I have to look into it. I guess I may have to attend law school here and take additional courses, and then I have to take an exam before I can practice or work for a law firm." Malathi sighed. " I want to straighten out this place first, Mangala." She continued," I need to get to get lot of new furniture for the house. We need new draperies. We need new appliances. I don't know how I can clean the house! You know back in India we had servants taking care of this! We even had a cook!! How do you take care of your place?"

"Oh! We have a Polish lady that comes twice a week and takes care of all the cleaning!! Polish are good housekeepers. Maybe I can have her see you."

"That will be great, Mangala! Also, can you tell me where to go for good furniture? You probably know real good ones around here."

"No problem, Malathi. I have my own car and I don't have any little kids at home. Sab works very hard being a neurosurgeon!! I can take you shopping till you get you own car!!" Mangala smiled.

"I am going to tell Raj that I am doing this. I am sure he won't mind! Let's go and see what the men are up to!!" Mangala went to the backyard.

Chapter Forty

Mangala came to the driveway in her Mercedes convertible. She had just gotten the brand new car as a birthday gift from her husband!

"He can afford it because he is a neurosurgeon," Malathi thought to herself. "What about Raj? Will he ever be able to do something nice like that?" She was not sure especially with the alimony and the child support Raj had to comply with.

"Are you Ready Malathi? I am going to take you to this furniture place you are really going to like. They have some gorgeous furniture you should see!"

"I am looking forward to this Mangala! Thank you for doing this for us. I told Raj that you are helping me pick out the sofa and kitchen cabinet. He is O.K. with it."

They arrived at Ethan Allen furniture showroom on Sheridan drive. The place was huge. Malathi was amazed to see the collection of beautiful pieces of furniture. One piece was better than the other! They both wandered around the store with a saleslady following them, showing them various collections.

Malathi liked a Victorian style sofa and a matching love seat. The velvety red color of the fabric was very striking. Eight hundred dollars for the two pieces!

" I am not sure if we can afford this, Mangala! I have to check with Raj!"

"Oh! Come on!! He is a surgeon. He can pay this off if he does one appendix surgery, Malathi!! I am sure he won't mind." Mangala was convincing.

"I suppose that makes sense. Let's look for the kitchen cabinet also."

Again the saleslady was very helpful. They looked at a dark mahogany cabinet with fancy stained glass doors and both agreed that would be perfect. That was on special sale for twelve hundred dollars only! Raj had given her the American Express credit card to use. Malathi used the card to pay for the furniture.

"You can expect delivery tomorrow, Mrs. Raj. I am sure Doc will be very pleased with your selections. What do you think, Mrs.Sab?"

Mangala smiled, "I am sure glad we came here. I always like the stuff I buy from here! You can't go wrong! Thanks for the help, Linda! See you soon!" They said goodbye to Linda, the saleslady and got in the car.

"Let's stop at Fanny's restaurant, Malathi! We are very close to the place. We can have some lunch. O.K.?"

"Yeah! I am getting a little hungry! What do they have? Anything special for lunch?"

Mangala had taken her other lady friends to Fanny's frequently.

"Oh, they have everything! Great salad and their garlic bread is out of this world!! If you like sea food, they have great crusted sea bass!!"

"That sounds good. Maybe I should ask Raj to try this place. I know he doesn't get time for lunch. That is a surgeon for you!! I am sure you are in the same boat. Right?" Malathi laughed.

"You know what, Malathi? I am so glad that I met you! We have a bunch of girls from Bombay and we get together once a week for lunch! I would like if you can join the group. You will get to know the others and you won't feel lonely!!"

Chapter Forty-One

"Hi! Honey! How did it go with Mangala today?" Raj asked Malathi after he gave her a kiss and removed his jacket and tie. He had an exhausting day at the hospital. Four tough cases to handle. He had trouble dealing with the family members who were not willing to accept the fact that their mother had been diagnosed with stomach cancer and surgery was not going to cure this. She needed more treatment like radiation and chemotherapy. Finally he was able to convince the family.

"It was really great Raj! You should see what I bought for us! The furniture is outstanding and I only spent less than two thousand dollars!!"

Raj's jaw dropped but he contained his emotions.

"That is still quite an expensive purchase, Honey. You know I have to watch all our spending at least for sometime till I am done with paying alimony!!"

"You can always do more surgery, right? Sabharwals have everything!! You have seen their home. I understand we can't be like them tomorrow! But in time, I am sure we can be better than them someday if we try."

"I do want you to be happy here with me, Honey. I know I will do my best. I will keep on working harder than ever to keep our family safe and secure."

"You know, Raj, after the shopping we went to Fanny's restaurant and had a great lunch. The manager, Mike, really knows Mangala well!! She even got a kiss on the cheek when he greeted us. I guess she and her other girl friends from Bombay go there often. That is a nice place. Maybe we should go for lunch someday!"

"It is always hard for me to take off for lunch. You know that. Most of the time I am in surgery!"

"Well, maybe one day you can take off. Ask one of your buddies to take care of patients. You are always covering for them! Right?"

"I suppose I can ask someday! Right now if I don't work, I don't make any money, Hon!!"

"She also wants me to meet the other girls from Bombay. I think she said she will have them for lunch at her place next Thursday. I am invited also. I was thinking of making some masala bath with vegetables and treating them. What do you think?"

"That sounds O.K. But right now I am hungry. Shall we order a pizza from Bocce's? It is too late for you to start cooking!!"

Chapter Forty-Two

"Hey! Raj, where have you been? I have been looking for you. I know you have a new wife now and are busy! But I wanted to tell you that my horse is running this Saturday at the Hamburg race track. I thought you could make some money! I know you could use some extra cash! Right ?" Dr.Barone had missed seeing Raj at the race track.

"I have not been to the race track since my divorce, Dr.Barone! I am not sure I can tell my new wife about this!" Raj was hesitant to commit.

"You know there is quarterly staff meeting this Saturday. You can tell her you are going to come home late." Dr. Barone had already thought of an excuse!

"Yeah! I also want to get away a little. Maybe it will be good for me!"

"O.K., Raj. I will see you at the hospital parking lot Saturday afternoon, and I can drive you to the track. How does that sound ?"

"Great! Doc! I will meet you Saturday!" Raj said goodbye and headed home.

On the way home Raj was thinking about what happened during surgery that morning.

"Hey Raj! I missed seeing you." He felt a tap on his shoulder when scrubbing. That was Brenda, his surgical nurse! She had been off for four weeks after falling on ice and breaking her leg. Raj had missed her very much.

"Oh! My God!! You are back! Brenda!! How is that leg of yours holding?"

"It is almost back to normal, Raj! I heard your new wife is here now!! How is that going for you?"

"You know how that is Brenda. I still have to get to know her. She is a lawyer, or I should say was a lawyer in India. Right now she is home and exploring her options"

"Well good for her! Dr. Sabharawal told me that his wife likes your wife!" Word travels fast! Raj thought to himself!

"They went and bought some furniture for our house. They sure have expensive taste!!"

"I suppose you have to work harder now! But try and take it easy, Raj! Maybe we can have a drink sometime after work!" She said with a sexy smile.

Raj sighed " I don't think that is going to happen, Brenda, as much as I'd love to!

Raj finished scrubbing and put on his surgical gloves given by Brenda and adjusted the mask.

The rest of the surgery went smoothly and Brenda made it a point to be as close to Raj as possible.

Chapter Forty-Three

"Honey! I have some great news for you!! Are you ready for this?" Malathi looked at Raj with a teasing smile.

"Yeah! What is it? Did you buy something for me? I know you were going shopping with Mangala!"

"No! Silly!! Remember I have been feeling a little tired and have been sick in the mornings!!"

"Oh! My God!! Honey, we are going to have a baby!!" Raj was excited and gave Malathi a big bear hug and kissed her affectionately on her lips.

"Yes! Anoop is going to have a baby brother or sister. We have to find out!" "I will talk to Dr. Jack Bartels and you can see him. He is the best. O.K.?"

"O.K. You can call him. I will go and see him. Now we have to work on another bedroom for the baby."

"We have the bedroom all set. We have to buy some baby furniture. I know you don't have any now!"

"I know! Lynette took the baby stuff!! What can I do? I had no choice."

"I will talk to Mangala. I am sure she will know where to fmd good baby furniture!"

"Maybe we can look for garage sales or moving sales. Sometimes we can get good stuff for cheap!" Raj knew he had to be watching the wallet!!

"Not too cheap, Honey! This is my first baby! I want the best for him or her" "Of course! I didn't mean real cheap furniture. Oh! You know what I mean?"

"Just remember! Your son from the other wife had everything!! At least I want the same for this child as well. That's all I am asking!! O.K.?"

"I get it, Malathi! Let's enjoy the evening!! What do you feel like eating?" "Why don't we go for some cinnamon ice cream! I have that craving!!"

"Great! There is this place in Williamsville called the Mill. They have the best cinnamon ice cream I have ever tasted!! Let's go there."

"Go ahead and get ready while I make a call to Jack and make your appointment with him for tomorrow." Raj went to the phone and Malathi went upstairs.

"Hey! Jack! I have good news for you. My wife is pregnant and she would like to see you. How about tomorrow afternoon?"

"O.K.! Raj! Congrats to you both. I think if she comes close to four I should be done with other patients. I can spend some time with her. Probably we will be doing the sonogram depending on how far along she is!" Jack was best at his specialty!

"No problem, Jack! I will have her see you tomorrow and my neighbor lady will bring her. You know her too! That is Sabharwal's wife!"

"Oh! Yes! Who doesn't know them!!, Jack laughed!

He is a nice guy though!!" Jack said bye and hung up the phone.

Malathi came down. Raj noticed a very special glow about her and felt very happy about having another addition to the family.

Chapter Forty-Four

The delivery room nurses were ready for Dr. Bartels. He had been quite busy with four deliveries earlier. Malathi was in full labor and contractions were getting stronger and frequent.

"Where is that husband of yours?" Jack walked in to the labor room.

"He should be here shortly, Dr. Bartels. He was finishing a case in the operating room just a while ago," the nurse explained.

"I think you can do natural, Malathi! Let's try. If you need something I can ask our anesthesiologist to go epidural. O.K.?"

"Do whatever you have to, Doctor Jack! Just get the baby out!!" Malathi gently screamed.

"Here he is! You made it on time, Raj! Go hold her hand and let her push!!"

"All right, Jack! Here, Honey! I am here!! Just follow Jack's instructions!"

"Push, Malathi! Push!! I see the baby's head!! His dark hair!! Here he comes." Jack was as excited as the parents!! They heard the baby cry and the nurse handed the baby to Malathi, gently laying the baby on her chest!!

"Your son is very handsome, Raj!! You are lucky!! Now you have two boys."

"Thank you very much, Jack! I really appreciate your help." Raj had tears in his eyes.

Malathi was sobbing as well, with tears of joy running down her cheeks. "Have you thought of a name for the baby yet?" the nurse, Nancy, asked.

"Jitu!! Easy name to pronounce!! Don't you think?" Raj held the baby's soft little hands.

"That is a pretty name. He looks like his mother more so than the father." That was nurse Nancy's observation.

" I think he is a little of both," Jack compromised. He is healthy!! Maybe he will follow in his daddy's footsteps, right, Raj?"

"I don't even think about it, Jack! After all the problems with private practice, you think medical field is still good?" Raj was serious for a minute.

"Well, I know we all complain about our profession. But you know, do you ever think of doing something other than this? Not a chance!"

Dr. Bartels had been in practice for over twenty five years and had delivered hundreds of babies!!

"All right, Raj! I am all done here. I am sure you have a pediatrician picked out already. Right?"

"Yes, Jack! Dr. Richards, the same one that took care of Anoop."

"He is good! See you, Malathi, in my office in two weeks. O.K.? Enjoy the new baby!" Jack said goodbye and shook Raj's hand and left the room.

Baby was asleep and looked very peaceful on Malathi's chest. Raj bent down and kissed her and touched the baby's hair.

Chapter Forty-Five

"Honey! We have been invited to a party at Sabharwals this weekend! I guess there will be seven couples, most of them you probably know! At least the husbands. All the guys are from Bombay. You will love to meet them. We have to find a baby sitter for Jitu." Malathi sounded very enthusiastic.

"I don't know if I know them all, Dear! But Sabharwals and Patels I know. Oh! There is this nice girl next door that's in junior high, and she can do the baby sitting. I will call her. O.K.?"

"That is great! I am really looking forward to meeting all the family. We can talk about old times!" Malathi continued, you know they are going to have the dinner catered! Deep, from Taste Of India, is taking care of the whole thing. Isn't that great?"

"At least the food will be good!! I am all for it!!" Raj laughed.

"Maybe for Jitu's second birthday that is coming up soon, we can invite them all here and we can do the same thing! Right?"

"I don't think we have had any company since the baby was born! Now that we are settled it would be nice to invite our friends." Malathi pleaded.

"Yeah! I am sure someday we can do that dear! Right now, we still need some more furniture, etc. Hopefully I will get my monthly medicare payment checks soon. We can look for furniture."

"We can go to the same place that Mangala took me and get some decent chairs and a table."

"Well, we don't have to get everything from there you know! There is Flanigan's furniture place! They are a little less expensive but they also have good stuff!" Raj argued.

"They may. But I don't want to look cheap, Honey! You have been to their places and you have seen their furniture! We are not on welfare! You are a surgeon!!"

"I know, Dear! But they don't have all the obligations that I have! Remember I lost half of my stuff through divorce. But we are doing better and slowly coming back! That's all I am saying." Raj threw his hands up in the air.

"Of course I know that. If you have to work harder, so be it!! You can always take a part time job!! I am stuck with the baby at home! I can't look for work."

"Let's not talk about this for now! What are you taking with you to Sabharwals?" Raj wanted to change the subject.

"I think we will just take a couple of bottles of champagne and a case of beer. They like that. I know the ladies like some white wine. Do we have any chardonnay?"

"I will look in the cellar! I think I have some there. Let me go look." Raj slid down from the couch and went down.

Malathi was thinking about what to wear to the party!

Chapter Forty-Six

Raj and Malathi gave instructions to Kimmy, the babysitter, about Jitu and walked out the door. Jitu was busy playing with his toys. As they walked towards the neighbor's house they saw all the expensive cars lining the driveway. Cadillacs, Mercedes and Corvettes!! They were greeted by the Sabharwals.

"Come on in, Raj! Meet the rest of the group here. You know the Patels. These are the Hurleys. This is Desai. Hey! Everybody, this is Raj and his wife, Malathi."

Raj shook hands with the guys and nodded to the ladies with a smile. Malathi took a look around and saw what the ladies were wearing. Her eyes wandered around the expensive jewelry they were all showing off!! She herself, had picked out the most expensive, gorgeous wedding sari and wore the diamond necklace and bracelets. "Wow! You look great, Malathi. Can't tell you just had the baby not too long ago! Are you on a diet? Looks like you have lost weight!" said Mangala.

"Thank you for the compliment, Mangala! I try hard! I know I still have to lose another eight to ten pounds!" Malathi felt happy about the comment.

"Here are the other ladies. Let's go out and get acquainted and leave the guys to talk about football!!" Mangala stepped out to the back porch. It was almost like a Florida room! Beautifully decorated with tropical plants, and walls covered with expensive paintings. There was a display shelf lined up with sandalwood and ivory statues of Gods and Goddesses! The table top was made of marble. There was nice shiny silverware next to expensive china.

"Your place is beautiful, Mangala. You have decorated the place like a pro! I am very impressed! Malathi continued, "I hope someday we can work on our back porch and build something like this."

"I am sure you can! Let's have some snacks. Who wants white wine?" Mangala knew how to entertain.

Deep and his assistants were busy pouring drinks and serving a variety of Indian snacks.

"Hey! Deep!! The vegetable fritters are great. I like the hot and spicy coriander chutney!" Raj was enjoying his Johnny Walker scotch and soda!

"You know, Raj! You should become a member of Transit Valley Country Club! There is open membership this month and only twelve thousand a year! We can get together once a month for dinner. You can play tennis or golf, if you are interested! I think you should get out more and not take your work too seriously!" Sabharwal wanted Raj's reaction.

"That's all well and good, Sab! But you know, with a new wife and a new baby, I don't think it is possible for me at this stage! But I would love to! Some day!"

"I wanted to tell you this, Raj! They are looking for a doctor to be on call at nights at the Psychiatric Center in West Seneca. I guess, twice a week. Really, there is no work at night. But you have to be there in case of emergency. Check them and send them to the nearest hospital if need be! I hardly got a call when I was on duty! You can certainly do that. That will give you some spending cash! Right?"

"You are right, Sab! I think I will stop there tomorrow and get the details and maybe I can sign up for two nights a week. Thanks for letting me know about this." Raj was indeed looking for a chance to make some more money.

Chapter Forty-Seven

Malathi wanted the birthday party to be a statement to the rest of her friends. She could host a great party and upstage everyone else, and she was determined to do this. She had sent out printed invitations to fifteen Indian families including her Bombay crowd! By the replies, it looked like almost all were coming!!

"Honey! I am so excited! I think we will have about forty to fifty people for Jitu's birthday party!! What do you think? That is bigger than the Sabharwals' party! Raj noted her excitement!

"O.K., Dear! Now, we have to make arrangements for catering. I know I can call Deep from Taste Of India and have him prepare the food. You can suggest the menu."

"Yeah! That's no problem. I am going to have him prepare a chicken dish, a lamb dish and maybe a lobster dish. We will have a big birthday cake. We will have some gulab jamun and mango ice-cream. Maybe, for the kids we can order a pizza! How does that sound?"

"I like that. tandoor chicken, lamb Madrasi will be good. With tandoor lobster we can have scallops makhani! Tell him to make them spicy!!" Raj added his suggestions.

"I am sure he will have biriyani rice and some okra masala along with pickles, pappadam and chutney! I can't wait!! Make sure you get home early from work this Friday!"

"I do have three cases scheduled that day, but I should be home by three! I can help you with cleaning and things! O.K.?" Raj knew that he had to be home well before the party got underway.

"I am also going to get some small gifts for the kids. Maybe some toys or books!" Malathi wanted to really impress the ladies!!

She already had a feeling that all would go well and she would come out on top!! Until now Mangala was in command of all the Bombay elite but now Malathi had a chance to take that spot. Even in college she wanted to be the professor's favorite, and she always liked other girls and guys hovering over her.

"Malathi! You are the best! You were the best student president! You are going to be the best lawyer!!" She was quite used to hearing these words back in India! Here, things were different. She knew that Raj had nowhere the income that other husbands were earning. She also knew that if she pushed him hard enough Raj would be able to bring in that kind of money!

"O.K.! Honey! I am going next doors and talk to Mangala for some suggestions for the party. You have food in the fridge and you can heat in the microwave. Jitu is still sleeping. You can watch him! I will be back soon." Malathi did not wait for an approval from Raj and went out the door.

Malathi was ecstatic about the outcome of the big birthday party. By everyone's standards this was outstanding. She had pleased the Bombay crowd and she had clearly proven herself as an equal among the elite!

"You did wonderful, Malathi. We all enjoyed the evening and we had so much fun! All the kids had a great time too." Mangala was all praises for Malathi. Malathi was on cloud nine! The only disappointment for her was that Raj was not making as much money as the other doctors. On numerous occasions she would bring up the topic.

"You know, Honey! You can also buy a Cadillac if you can work a little harder!"

"Then you won't see me at home! You would have to be in charge of Jitu and maybe of Anoop, if he spends the time with us this summer!"

"But! But! How are they all able to handle the finances and not you!"

"Dear! You don't understand! They have no worries! Their kids are grown up! They also come from rich families back in India. My family was not rich, by any means." Raj almost lost his patience.

"You know, I am going to the psychiatric center tomorrow and sign up for two nights a week on call service. Maybe that will give me a few more bucks!"

"That will be good, Raj! Maybe I can buy that necklace I looked at the other day at the Indian Bazaar!"

"You will have to wait till I get paid first!! I have not even started work yet." "I can wait, Dear, so long as you promise me you will do this for me!!" "Let's not put the cart before the horse! Let me see if I get the job!"

Raj put his jacket and shoes on and walked into the garage.

He was happy to get out of the house! He had a busy day of surgery at the hospital. His bright part of the day was seeing Brenda and work with her closely. Just thinking about her, slight shiver went though his spine!

He knew she was very attracted to him and had mentioned several times how much she would love to have a drink with him. He parked his car in the doctor's parking lot and went to the staff room. It was still early but the coffee pot was ready and so were some bagels and donuts.

He grabbed a bagel and after separating the halves dropped them in the toaster. He liked them dark. In the little fridge there was cream cheese and half & half. He poured himself a cup of coffee, added two teaspoons of sugar and the half & half. The bagel tasted good with the fresh cream cheese. He looked at the headlines of the Buffalo News and more bad news for the city. Republic steel mill was closing. After the grain mill had been closed, now this! No one knows what's in store!

After sipping his last drop of coffee he slowly got out and headed to the operating room.

Chapter Forty-Eight

"Hey! Raj! You have been very quiet this morning. Is everything O.K.?" Brenda was really noticing the change. Raj was always jovial and talkative during surgery.

"What can I tell you Brenda? I am being constantly nagged at home by my dear wife! I guess I don't work as hard as the other doctors. She would love us to keep up with the Joneses. You know what I mean?" Raj was not holding back his feelings.

"I can understand that, Raj! Especially since she has been surrounding herself with these other ladies! All they talk about is about who has what and how much!!"

"You can see that, but why can't she? Hand me the suture Brenda!"

"You should do what is best for you! You can't kill yourself! Life is too short!"

"I am going to be working twice a week at the psychiatric center in West Seneca Brenda, starting next week! That will get me out of the house for a while!!"

"I am going to be off next Friday, Raj! Why don't we go for a drink and just talk!!"

Brenda was very sincere. She was very concerned that Raj looked very depressed. If there was something she could do to make him feel any better, she was willing to do it. She always admired his surgical skills and she wanted to see him smiling again.

"Yeah! Brenda! I can tell my wife that I got an emergency call and can leave the house early on Friday. How about if I come to your place about five?"

Brenda's face lit up and she slightly blushed. Raj thought she looked more attractive this morning for some reason. After the case was finished he let the assistant finish the dressing and walked to the linen room. He heard the footsteps following him. It was Brenda! She held his hand and grabbed him closer and gave him a big kiss. Raj enjoyed every second of this experience and hoped it would last longer!! He held her tight and kissed her with passion. He had never felt this way since the very first time he had gone out on a date with Lynette, his first wife.

"All right, Doc! Let's get back to work! We can save some of this for later!!" Brenda winked and went back to the operating room.

"My God! What a feeling! A rush of endorphins!, Can't wait till Friday!" Raj caught himself softly whistling!!

The rest of the morning went very smoothly. He felt the added energy and breezed through other cases.

"Hey, Raj! You look very happy! Did you win a lottery?" Dr. Bartels teased him as they met in the doctor's lounge.

"No! Jack! I wish I did! All my cases went very smooth today. No problems with any excess bleeding or other complications!!"

"That's always good news. How is that little boy of yours? What, he must be two now! Right?" Jack remembered.

"That's right, Jack! He is a big boy now!! We have our hands full!!" "Well, take it easy! See you tomorrow, Raj." Jack left the room.

Raj got in his car and his mind was all on Brenda. For once he could smile!

Chapter Forty-Nine

"Honey! Today is Friday. Remember, I am going out to dinner with the ladies, the Bombay group." Malathi reminded Raj.

"Of course I do! You guys have a great time. Make sure the babysitter, Kimmy, is available tonight dear! I may be late coming home myself!!" Raj had to contain his good feeling!

"I have already called Kimmy and she will be here to baby sit. Don't worry!"

"That's good. I am off to work!" Raj landed a quick kiss on Malathi's lips and entered the garage and got in his car. This will be a great day, he thought. He had been waiting to spend time with Brenda. He knew he would be picking her up later that evening. He had packed his electric shaver as usual and his favorite cologne! He liked Royal Copenhagen, and all the nurses at the hospital always commented how great he smells!!

He had scheduled three surgeries for that morning. He wanted to be free for the evening. He had arranged coverage for emergencies and his friend, Dr. White had made himself available. Raj had taken his calls several times in the past and this time it was Dr.White's turn to reciprocate. Raj didn't have to explain why he needed the coverage! He remembered telling Dr. White that he had an appointment with his financial advisor, Luca. No further discussions!

He got into the operating room and noticed a substitute scrub nurse, Lindsey. He had worked with her before. This one was much older and not as friendly as Brenda.

"Hi! Lindsey! It's going to be a nice day, right?" Raj greeted her.

"Yeah! The weatherman says we may hit seventy today!! We need some warmer weather. I am getting sick of cloudy, cold weather which is depressing!"

"I agree, Lindsey! Nice to have clear blue skies and warm sunshine for a change! Let's get to work, Lindsey! By the way, I am supposed to have a surgical resident assisting me also. Is he here?"

"He will be a few minutes late, Doc! Stuart is his name and he is in his third year. He is good. He has worked with Dr. White and other surgeons, and you will like him."

"That's good. I don't mind working with senior residents. I love to teach them!"

Raj was considered to be a very good teaching attending. Young and upcoming surgeons liked the way he operated. Raj was not only fast but very meticulous at the same time.

"Sorry, Doctor Raj! Traffic was held up on the Skyway Bridge. Some construction problem, I guess!" Stuart had put on his mask and gloves and was ready to go!

"We are going to take the gallbladder out. This lady has had chronic disease and has had three acute attacks before. Gallbladder is full of stones. Let's do a right upper quadrant incision. Go ahead, you can start, Stuart!" Raj handed the scalpel. Surgery went very well. He had to make sure that there were no stones left in the duct carrying the bile. The radiologist injected dye and the duct was clean.

"Make sure you stay away from the big artery that feeds the liver!!" Raj pointed the spot.

Stuart was able to complete the closing after all the steps were followed.

"Make sure the instrument check is correct Lindsey! We don't want to leave any clamps inside the belly!!" Raj laughed and left the room to change.

After he finished the last case, Raj left instructions for the surgical resident and hurried out of the operating room. He ran into Dr. White near the doctor's lounge.

"You seem to be in a real hurry, Raj" he quipped.

"I am already late for my appointment with the financial advisor, John. I have to run." "O.K. Take it easy. I will take care of your calls."

Raj said good bye and got in his car and put his pedal to the metal! His Buick roared and hit the expressway to Brenda's house. She lived not too far from the hospital since she had to take calls frequently to assist in surgery.

Her house was located in a nice neighborhood. Most of the homes were single family homes. The development was fairly new, probably six or seven years old. There were treed lots with nice landscaping around. Some of the homes had good sized backyards. Raj pulled into the driveway. Brenda was waiting for him, watching through the window!

Even before he rang the door bell the door was open and there was Brenda with a great smile on her face. She greeted Raj with a hug and a long kiss on his lips.

Raj was excited to see her. She looked even more beautiful without the hospital garb! Beautiful curly blonde hair and her shiny bright blue eyes complemented her ivory complexion. Her body was like an art form. She could have been a model after all!

"Hey! Raj! You made it! I was afraid you might back off in the last minute."

"No way, Dear! I have been waiting for this moment ever since I had my eyes on you!"

Raj continued to hug and kiss her repeatedly. He had not felt this way before.

"What shall we do? Have a drink and then go to Orchard Downs for dinner?"

"That sounds good. I have your favorite scotch. Have a drink and then we can go." Brenda squeezed his hand and held it tight and led him to the family room.

Raj prepared the drinks for both.

"Cheers! Here's to us!!" Brenda touched her glass to his and took a sip.

"Cheers! Here is to good health and friendship, Brenda!!" Raj leaned and kissed her again. They sat on her love seat, bodies tight against each other's. Raj started caressing her gently and felt her flesh for the first time, smooth as silk. He was enjoying every second of this experience. Brenda ran her fingers through his hair and kissed him over and over.

"You are a great surgeon! I knew that! I didn't know you are a great lover too! Raj!. I am so glad you decided to spend time with me! I know you are not very happy with your wife. I am here for you, Honey! If you just need someone to talk, I am here!"

"I feel so much better already, Brenda. What I am doing is wrong but I have no choice." They stayed on the love seat for what felt like an eternity and started feeling hungry! Raj kissed goodnight to Brenda .

"I had a great time Brenda! This is one of my best days of my life! Thank you for everything! We can't do this often, as I am a married man! But I will try to be with you as much as I can. Hope you understand!" Raj kissed her again.

"Don't worry Raj, Dear! I am very deeply fond of you. I know I can't have you all the time. We are grownups! We can handle this. I really enjoyed being with you tonight! Thank you for the dinner and the great time together!! God willing, we will get together again!!" Raj could see Brenda was choking a bit and saw the tears running down her cheek. He gave her another hug and hopped in the car. Now he has to face the music! Malathi should be back by now from her dinner. He got home and the babysitter was still home.

Chapter Fifty

" Hey! Kimmy!! I guess my wife is not home yet. Did she call?"

"Hi, Doc. Yeah! She was going to stop at one of the lady's home and drop off something. She should be here any minute now! How was your meeting?"

"Good, Kimmy' By the way, I wanted to tell you how grown up you look in just two years! You are turning out to be a beautiful young lady!!"

Kimmy blushed and smiled.

"You know I love to baby-sit at your house any time." Kimmy was obviously attracted to Raj and the feeling was mutual.

"Maybe this summer you can work in my office. Help with filing, mailing and things like that! How do you like that?"

"Wow! That would be great. I will tell my parents. I am sure they would like it if I can earn some money!! I could always use some extra cash!!"

"O.K.! I will mention that to my wife also! Here she is! I hear the garage door open. O.K., Kimmy, you can leave We'll call you again."

Kimmy said goodnight to Malathi as she walked in and bolted out though the door! "Hi, Hon! How was your dinner with the ladies?" Raj broke the silence.

"It was great, dear! They all want me to be in charge of Independence Day celebrations. August 15th is the day. India association is having a special evening. They have music, entertainment, kids' games etc. I am supposed to supervise everything including the food!! They thought I am the best to oversee the entire affair!! What do you think?"

"That's very good for you, honey! I am sure you will enjoy doing this!" Raj could see how excited she was about this new leadership role.

Malathi never bothered to ask Raj how his day went!! She was in her own world!

"O.K.! It's getting late. Let me pour me a drink and let's hit the sack! I am tired!" Raj went to the bar and got himself a glass of scotch. He did not ask Malathi if she wanted anything to drink!

Chapter Fifty-One

"Honey! I am working at the psychiatric center tonight. I hope I don't get too many calls," Raj reminded Malathi.

"I am glad you started working there, dear. Now I think you can buy me that Ford Mustang I looked at the other day!! Malathi laughed, but she was serious.

"I won't get my paycheck till the end of the month. We will have to wait, Honey!"

"I will be so happy to have my own new car. I am tired of asking the other girls to give me a ride all the time."

"You know when we came to this country I had nothing but an empty wallet! I think it took two years before I bought an old car. That's all I could afford. Thank God, now I live in my own home and can buy some decent things for the family."

"How can other families do so well? There's got to be a secret to making money! Maybe they have a better financial advisor. Mangala was telling me that they may buy a cottage in crystal beach in Canada. We can't even afford to have two cars!"

"Good for them! Someday we may be able to do the same. I am trying hard, Hon." Raj did not want to prolong the debate with his lawyer wife. It was fruitless anyway!

"You know, next week I will have to be going with Anoop to look at colleges. That is another big expense coming up for us."

"I know you have to do it. You have no choice! Wish your ex could do some of this!"

"No! She works as a nurse in Rochester General Hospital. She can't take time off Since I am supporting his education I will have to do it. Our parents did for us. Without their sacrifices we wouldn't be where we are today." Raj was thinking of his father and could not hold back tears.

"All I am saying dear, just remember you have two other children to care for! I want the same for Jitu and Reena, also." Malathi left the room.

Raj shouted, "Of course, Dear! They are my kids too!!"

Raj had set up an educational trust fund for Anoop with the help of his financial advisor. At least, for a public college, there was enough in the funds to cover four years of tuition. Anoop was staying home with his mother and Raj didn't have to worry about lodging. Anoop had no interest in becoming a doctor but he always enjoyed technology and computers. Raj was very happy to encourage Anoop in whatever field he wanted to pursue and not push a medical career. Anoop was very close to his dad even though as son and father they did not have all the time they could have shared if there was no divorce. But there was quality time whenever he spent summer vacation with Raj. They would go to the Buffalo Bill's football games or Sabre's hockey games.

Anoop had a very pleasant personality and nothing seemed to bother him. He had lots of patience and got along with everybody. Even when there were tense moments with his step mother he never once complained to his father.

"Hi! Dad! I am very happy to let you know I got accepted at University Of Rochester," Raj was extremely happy to hear from his son.

"Too bad, you didn't want to take up medical field!" He thought to himself.

"I am so glad, Anoop. I know you will do great. I know you will be staying with your mother, but if you need assistance in getting books or whatever let me know. Four years will fly by before you know it!! I will celebrate the news with some of my friends."

"Thanks, Dad! I am sure I will concentrate on studies. As you know, I never got into any sports or anything! It must be your influence I guess!!" Anoop hung up the phone.

Raj thought of his buddy, Chandu, and realized he had not talked to him in ages! Even when there were parties with friends at home, Chandu or his other friends from Bangalore were excluded. Malathi was always jealous of Raj's mention of his close friends.

"You have spent a lot of time with them before! It is my time now. Now we have our new friends, our Bombay friends! You guys can meet at some medical meeting or other. Besides, your close buddy does not even bother calling me to find out how we are doing! To each his own," Malathi would argue with Raj.

That's one of the reasons he had not invited his close friends to any family functions.

"Hey, Chandu! I am sorry I have not called you sooner. But you understand! Anoop got accepted at University Of Rochester. I am very happy!"

Chandu was very much pleased to hear from his old buddy.

"Hey! What the hell is happening man? I don't think you know that I am still alive and kicking!!"

"Don't make me feel worse than I am already feeling, Chandu. You know what the story is here! The ladies rule!! I know you have been busy yourself I hear you have a girlfriend now! Is that true?"

"Yeah! This one looks like a keeper buddy!! I will tell you all about that if we can only meet somewhere. Is that even possible?"

"I was going to tell you. You know I work two nights a week at the psychiatric center. Now I got a job as a race track physician at the Hamburg race track. I work only on weekends either Friday night or Saturday night. It is nice work! All I do is sit and watch the races. If there is some injury to the jockeys or the trainers, I will have to check them and send them to the hospital, if need be. I get free dinner besides!!"

"That's right up your alley!! Don't tell me you are back into gambling your earnings away!! I hope not!" Chandu always knew his friend's weakness.

"I do gamble a little! Not like before, to be honest with you. Oh! the reason I mention this, we can meet this Friday evening at the race track and catch up with our lives!! What do you say?"

Chandu had missed his companion for an extended period of time. He had his own issues that he wanted off his chest. This would be perfect.

"O.K.! Brother! I will see you al the track Friday evening. Look for me."

Raj somehow felt very comforting thinking about seeing his buddy after a long time!

Chapter Fifty-Two

"Hey! Malathi! I will have to work at the race track to-night. I will be having dinner there. Don't wait up for me. You guys eat. I probably won't be home till eleven thirty tonight. O.K.?" Raj reminded his wife.

"That's fine with us, Dear! At least you will be making some money! Just don't lose it on horses!!" Malathi laughed. "By the way we have to pick up my new car next week and I hope you have talked to your financial advisor, Luca, have you?"

"Yes, I did, Honey! He says leasing is the way to go rather than buying it outright. We only have to come up with the down payment and one month's lease payment," Raj explained.

"Whatever you and him do, that is fine with me! I just get my car!! Oh! By the way, the New York Life Insurance agent called and he wants to make an appointment with you some time next week. You have to do that too! Don't forget, O.K.?"

Raj just remembered the talk he had with Luca and he had strongly advised Raj to buy life insurance enough to cover the cost of home mortgage, children's education and wife's life time expenses in case something were to happen to Raj! He had suggested a minimum of million dollar whole life insurance. Since Raj was still young, the premiums would be very afford-able. He liked the idea very much and was going to follow through.

When he got to the racetrack Chandu was waiting at the club house on time.

"Hello! Chandu! Hope you brought some gambling money with you!! I can give you some good tips about the horses," Raj laughed!!

"Are you kidding? I left my wallet at home!! I need all the money I can get to buy an engagement ring for my girlfriend!" Chandu gave a hug to his buddy he had not seen in months.

"O.K.! Let's order drinks and we can order our dinner later! Tell me about your girlfriend. Where is she from and where did you meet her?" Raj was curious.

"Well, she comes from a very small town near Ithaca, New York. Her father is a Vet who takes care of small animals and her mother is a teacher. They have a large farm and I guess they grow corn and things. Lucy is their daughter and she is a nurse at the Emergency Hospital in downtown. I have been an attending there and I have started an endoscopy room adjacent to the ER. When I do procedures, she helps me with the meds, etc. She is a blonde and you know how both of us fall for blondes!!" Chandu laughed.

"So, I take it you asked her out and she said yes! Is that it? How long have you been dating this girl?"

"We have been going out for the past two months. Mostly dinners and movies, you know! But I guess this July Fourth, the family has a picnic at the cottage they own by Cayuga lake. She wants me to come to the picnic and meet the parents! I am really thinking about this."

"Hey! What the heck! What's there to think about? You should go and have a good time! What parent does not want their daughter to marry a doctor! Especially a great gastroenterologist making tons of money!! Right?" Raj was teasing.

"I am anxious to meet the family too! From what I hear, her mother is very friendly and her father is some what strict and regimented!! She has three brothers."

"Let's order our dinner, Chandu! You will like their Beef on Week here."

Chapter Fifty-Three

Raj had hired Kimmy to do the filing job at the office. She was very delighted that she could be with him and was looking forward to this day.

"I see you are here early, Kimmy! This is Chris, my office manager. She will show you the ropes! O.K.? If you have any questions you can always ask me!" Raj was very happy to see her. She was now in college as a freshman at University Of Buffalo. She was interested in studying psychology.

"You should look into getting to medical school, Kimmy, " Raj had told her few times.

"No! I see how hard you work night and day and twenty four seven!! No! I don't think I can do that, Raj!" That was the first time she called him by his name instead of calling him Doc!!

"That's much better Kimmy! You can call me Raj! I have known you at least for the past four years I think!!" Raj pinched her chin and stroked her face gently and Chris was out of sight at that time!

Kimmy blushed and felt warm all over. This was what she was dreaming of!

"I like you very much, Kimmy! I know you will be a good worker here. Oh, by the way I can take you home if your parents can't pick you up! You live right down the street! O.K.?

"Thank you, Raj. If I need a ride I sure will take up the offer. Now tell me what do you want me do first."

"Go with Chris. She will start you off with filing lab reports in patient's charts."

Kimmy got busy and patients started rolling in. She was very impressed about the way he was taking care of them.

"I have a call from your wife, Raj. She says it is urgent and she must talk to you ." Chris buzzed her boss.

"O.K. I will take the call right after I am done with this patient. Put her on hold or keep talking to her! Will you?" Raj was taking the sutures off from a patient he had performed partial gastrectomy for a bleeding ulcer. The patient, Roger, was doing very well.

"Thank you very much, Doc, for saving my life! If I didn't have you to fix my stomach, I guess I would have been a goner!! My wife and kids thank you too, for giving my life back." Roger shook Raj's hands and walked over to Chris to take care of the bill.

"Hi, Honey! What is the emergency? Everything O.K.? Raj was anxious.

"Everything is 0.K, Dear. I got a call from Dr. Prasad's office. He wants you to call him as soon as you can! I guess he wants to discuss about your blood work. Call him."

Malathi knew Raj had gone for a routine check up with his internist last week.

"1 will call his office right now. My next patient is not due for another fifteen minutes." He hung up the phone.

"This is Dr. Raj. I understand Dr.Prasad has been looking for me." He told the secretary.

"Oh, Yes! Dr. Prasad will be right with you, Doc. I will pull your chart." Dr.Prasad's voice was some what somber.

"Hey! Raj! Did any one in your family have diabetes?"

"My grandfather had type -2. Why?" Raj was shaken.

"You are also a type-2. Your fasting blood sugar came back high. Looks like you have to go on a diabetic diet and maybe an oral diabetic drug."

Chapter Fifty-Four

"You know, Malathi! I think Chandu and his wife, Lucy, came back from their honeymoon from Hawaii. We should have them over for dinner sometime. What do you think?" Raj asked his wife and waited for the answer.

"Well, Dear! They just got back and I am sure they have tons of things to do at home! After all they are just settling down. He married an American girl!

I am not sure how much she likes our company or our food!!" Malathi was not too enthusiastic about having them just yet!

"Well! I just thought it would be nice to invite them for a cocktail at least! But if you feel you are not ready, so be it! We will wait!" Raj walked out of the room.

"Raj! Don't forget we are going to Dr. Desai's house this Saturday. They have invited us for a birthday party for his wife. I have to do some shopping. I am thinking of giving her some piece of jewelry. My neighbor, Mangala, is going with me. 0.K? She shouted out so that Raj could hear her.

Raj had been started on a diabetic diet and put on pills to control his blood sugar. He was supposed to monitor his own blood sugar levels twice a day with the glucometer. Even though as a doctor he had advised hundreds of patients to do this, he himself thought it was a pain in the neck!! But he had no choice! He had been watching sugar intake and calories. He had bought an exercise tread mill and some weight lifting equipment and started using them in the basement game room. Physically he felt better, but he felt depression creeping in at times. The pressures of being in private practice and having to work two other jobs to take care of the family needs were overwhelming at times.

The liability insurance company had increased their premium for surgeons by thirty percent. Now that Anoop was in college, there were additional costs although the tuition was not a major problem. His son, Jitu, was now in high school and he would be ready for college in two years. He had indicated interest in pursuing a medical career. Raj was very happy about that, but it meant huge expenses still to come.

His daughter, Reena, was Daddy's girl all the way! Her temperament was very much like her daddy and he always would give in to her wishes.

"You complain about me, Dear, that I spend a lot! You are spoiling your own daughter. You can't say 'No' to her!!" Malathi would tease him.

"Well, her stuff doesn't cost an arm and a leg like yours does!!" Raj would counter argue!

Raj had not gone out with Brenda again after that one great time he spent with her. His mind was also was wandering thinking about Kimmy. She had turned out to be a buxom, beautiful young lady, He knew he could ask her out anytime!

If only he could win a big trifacta at the race track that could change his life!

Chapter Fifty-Five

Erie County Medical Society had their annual meeting at the Marriott Hotel, which is located in Amherst, NY, on Millersport Highway. Raj was happy to be out of the house and he knew that Chandu would be there also. Chandu had indicated there were things very important he had to discuss. Raj had no clue as to what that might be. After all, Chandu had been married almost eleven years and had three beautiful daughters ranging in ages eleven to three. Chandu had recently gone to India to attend the anniversary of the death of his stepmother. His aging father had been devastated by the loss and now he had been staying with his second son, an attorney in Bangalore. Chandu's father had insisted on staying in his own home in a small town about sixty miles from Bangalore.

After much coaxing he was convinced staying alone was not a good idea at his age. All the boys and the only girl always admired their stepmother for all the sacrifices the two of them had made to raise the children. Chandu's mother died of complications after delivering the baby girl she had been wishing for after having five boys! She died of massive postpartum hemorrhage. Chandu was barely ten years old and he was the middle one! Raj remembered Chandu telling him the story about how all the kids went on a hunger strike when their father announced he was going to remarry!!

"Go right ahead! If you guys get hungry you will eat! I don't care if you go without food! Who is going to take care of you everyday? Cook for you, take care of the house?" I guess the strike didn't lost long!! After they met their stepmother and found out more about her family and the way she took care of Dad, they were completely in her corner. She never had any children of her own. I guess five boys and a girl were a handful!!

"Hey! I have been looking for you! You look like hell! What is wrong?" Raj could see Chandu had dark circles under his eyes. He looked like he had no sleep for days.

"Let's go to the corner table. I am in deep shit!! My wife dropped a bombshell on me and my family!! As you know, I just got back from India. I had trouble calling home to tell Lucy when I would get back. You know how much of a problem it is to call from India, not to speak of how much it costs to call! I had to take a bus from the Toronto Airport to get home. I come home and I see Lucy. Not a hug, not a kiss!! She quietly tells me that she is going to file for divorce! I thought she might be just mad that I was gone to India and not contact her while there. But, No!! She was serious. After the kids went to bed, she told me she has decided to leave me!"

"Did she have someone else?" Raj was in shock to hear this.

"No! Buddy! Not that I know of! She says 'I have to find myself.' What the hell that means, God knows! If she doesn't know who she is at her age and after three kids, what is wrong with this picture, Raj!" Chandu could no longer hold back tears. "She has already seen an attorney from a big divorce law firm and I am sure I will be getting the papers. I am totally screwed!! How can I explain this to the young kids? This is the worst day of my life, Raj! I hope you stick with me if I need you!"

"Of course! You can count on me, Chandu! You were there for me when I went through the same with Lynette! You will survive this, by God's grace!!" Raj held his friend's hand tight. They had two glasses of scotch to calm their nerves.

Chapter Fifty-Six

Chandu got a phone call from Dr.Prabhakar. This was a surprise since he had not spoken to him in several months.

"Hey! What's up, buddy? I don't even know if you are still in town!" Chandu laughed.

"The reason I am calling, our friend, Raj, has been hospitalized at Mercy hospital. I am not sure what is wrong. I am going to see him at the hospital this evening. You want to go with me?"

"Of course! You want to come to my place and one of us can drive. O.K.?" Chandu had not talked to Raj in over a week. He knew Raj was a diabetic and the medications, diet and exercise had kept things well under control. Malathi never bothered to call Chandu, although she had contact with Prabhakar. She felt very comfortable with him and his wife, Sudha, who was from Mysore, India.

Prabhakar arrived on time in his Mercedes, and Chandu greeted him atthe door. Chandu's children were with their mother for the weekend. Since he had joint custody, they would alternate the weekends taking care of them.

"You want a beer?" Chandu offered.

"No, since I will be driving, I don't want to take a chance! I know one beer may not do anything! But I can't trust the cops!! Especially when we are doctors!!"

"That's fine! Let me make you some coffee! I have some snacks from India I have saved!! Let's munch!" Chandu brought out a plate of crunchy spicy snacks.

They sipped coffee and Chandu got on the passenger side of Prabhakar's Mercedes.

They arrived at the hospital and got on the elevator to the sixth floor. Raj was in a private room on the medical floor.

"Hey! What the heck happened to you? Did you want to take some time off from work!! Really! Did they tell you what is wrong?" Chandu sat by the bed and shook Raj's hand.

"No! Guys! Nothing serious! I kind of had mild flu symptoms last week and yesterday morning when I was going down the basement stairs I must have slipped and fallen down, hitting my head. I was not out or anything! But to be sure, my wife thought I should come to E.R.! They have x-rayed me! They did a CT scan of my head! I still have all my marbles!!" Raj laughed out loud.

"Thank God for that!! You had us scared!! You've got to be more careful going down those stairs," Prabhakar added.

"I suppose so! Anyway, they are going to observe me one more night and send me home tomorrow! I guess I needed a little R & R!! I thank you guys for comingl!"

"You should take the rest of the week off, boy! Take it easy for now! We will get going! Good night, buddy!" Chandu got up and shook Raj's hand and stroked his head.

"I will call you guys sometime! But if you don't hear from me, you know, no news is good news!! Good night!" Raj bid goodbye to his buddies.

His mind was on the events of that morning! A strange sensation flashed through and he was quietly sobbing.

Chapter Fifty-Seven

Raj was just finishing up his paper work at the office when he got a call from Chandu.

"Hey! Raj, my boy! I have some good news for you for a change!! Are you ready?" "You sound very excited, buddy! What's new?" Raj was curious.

"Remember, I told you that I had met this great blonde who is working for our weight loss program that our hospital has started?"

"Yeah! You said she has been married and has two kids! Right?"

"That's the one I am talking about. She smokes a lot and that is the only thing that bothers me! Another girl that works there mentioned to Kay, that's her name, I was interested in going out with her but told her that I hate smokers!!"

"So, what happened? Did you ask her out?"

"There was a party at the Red Carpet restaurant for a staff member who is going to retire. Actually, when the staff asked me to come to the party, I asked Kay if she was going to the party! When she said yes, I told her that I could pick her up on the way! So, I did!!"

"How did that work out? Did you guys hit it off?"

"It was like, like, Hum! Love at first sight!! I was attracted to her the very first time my supervisor introduced her!! I knew right then and there, she was the one for me!!"

"I take it the feeling was mutual! You know the saying 'once bit- twice shy'!!" Raj laughed.

"She has great personality, a little shy, I must say! We had a great time. We even danced!!" Chandu sounded very happy.

"I am very, very happy for you Chandu! What about her smoking? Doesn't that bother you? What about your kids? What do they think?"

"Well, I have to slowly work on it! My kids have met her a couple of times. They like my choice! My first two girls are almost the same age as her daughter and son."

"Has she been officially divorced or just separated?"

"I guess the divorce is in the works! Not final yet, I guess! I can wait."

"Where does she live now? Does she have the kids with her?"

"Yeah! She lives in Kenmore with her kids. They go to school there. She worked for the lab at the hospital as a phlebotomist. Now she does that and also does other things like EKG tech and secretarial work as well!!"

"That really sounds great, Chandu! Maybe we should go out to dinner together." "I would love to have you and Malathi meet her, for sure!"

"I am glad you called me. Let me know how things progress! O.K.! Buddy!!"

"Of course you will be the first to know, boy! I am going to sit down with my girls tonight and let them know how I feel about Kay!! I want them to like her and I want my kids to get to know her kids! I think they will get along fine, being the same age! My little one is only three years old and I don't think she really, knows what is happening!"

"I know, I only had one kid before I got married again! You have three!! It is not going to be easy raising the kids!! Too bad both of us have to face this in life!"

"You know what? God has His ways! For everything that happens in life there is - always a reason, right? See you soon, Raj!" Chandu hung up the phone.

Raj's mind wandered back to the days when the two were in Madras and ran into the palmist who had predicted some unhappy events.

Chapter Fifty-Eight

Chandu and Kay had a wonderful time on their cruise to the Caribbean Islands.

The best thing was, Kay had her last cigarette before she boarded the flight to Florida to catch the cruise ship. She had done very well going cold turkey and Chandu was very proud of her!

Now that he was back to work he was thinking of making some changes in his office personnel. Dawn had worked for him as his secretary for nearly fifteen years. She had trouble dealing with some of the patients, especially female patients who were very fond of Chandu. He had observed her manners and this was not acceptable.

Chandu always wanted his office to run very smooth and efficient. Nobody waited in his office more than fifteen minutes, and he always gave them enough time to be properly examined and treated. That's what had made his name very popular in the community, and he had earned the respect of his colleagues and friends.

Most of the family physicians referred their patients with digestive diseases to Chandu and they knew he would come up with the best plan of care.

"I wouldn't send him to anyone but Dr.Chandu!" Most of them would say! Chandu was humble and always sent an appreciation note to the referring doctors. He also had a great working relationship with the nurses at the hospital.

He always treated them with respect and was eager to teach them, even if it took a little longer to do the procedure. He had trained many of the new nurses and they were very grateful for the opportunity to have worked with him.

The week before the super bowl, was always special. Chandu would take all the nurses and their husbands to Taste Of

India restaurant and treat them to a great Indian gourmet meal!!
Every year, the staff would look forward to this event.
This was "Chandu's party!!"

"We don't know what we'll do after you retire!! We are
going to miss this very much," Marcy would say! Chandu liked to
work with her since she was a very good assistant.

"Dawn! I want to talk to you. I know you just came back
after your maternity leave. The temp I had during your absence
had a very tough time doing the office billing. You never left her
any instructions on how to code or prepare the billing! I was very
much disappointed! You have been with me almost fifteen years,
Dawn! Now even some of my patients are complaining about
how you treat them over the phone when they call the office. I
don't know what is happening with your life. But I am sorry!
I think I will have to let you go. I will give you excellent recommendations if you look for a new position. I have asked my wife,
Kay, to start working here in your place. I would appreciate if you
can show her the ropes. I know you were with me when I went
through my difficult divorce." Chandu choked up a little!

"I am sorry, Chandu! I have worked only for you and I
feel a strong connection with you and your life! I am going to
miss you very much. I will do my best to teach your wife, Kay,
whatever I know!" Dawn was overcome with emotions and tears
rolled down her cheek. She wept quietly for a few minutes.
Chandu held her close for a short second and gave a soft kiss on
her forehead.

"O.K. I have to go to the hospital to see a consult! Take
care, Dawn!!" Chandu went out through the back door.

Dawn felt like she was struck by lightening. She picked
up the phone and called Dick, her husband, who was watching the
baby.

Chapter Fifty-Nine

"I wonder who could be calling me at five in the morning, Kay!" Chandu grabbed the phone. Kay was deep asleep and she didn't even move!

"Hello, this is Dr.Chandu! Who is calling?" He could not recognize the voice at the other end for a split second! "Hey! It is you! Raj! What the hell are you doing up this early!"

"I could not sleep well, buddy! Now-a-days I am up at four or five in the morning! I am really worried about my finances, Chandu. My son, Jitu, is now in Boston going to medical school. He did not get any financial aid. The education fund I had set up for the kids is not enough to pay for this. As you know I am busting my ass, working three jobs and even that is not enough for Malathi! She keeps blaming that I don't know how to make money! My malpractice premium went up another twenty five percent!! How the hell am I going to survive? You tell me!!" Raj was very serious.

"Calm down, Raj! We all have the same problem. I have four kids in college at the same time. As you know, after the divorce I am down to half of everything I own! My ex took me to the cleaners! I am trying to build my life back again. I know it is not easy!! It never is!! But we have to hang in there for the sake of our kids and do the best we can, like our parents did for us!!"

"But, but! Boy! I feel helpless and hopeless, man! I feel so depressed sometimes that I don't even want to go to work! I am worried about my diabetes even though I am watching my diet and taking my meds. What would you do?" Raj was looking for answers.

"There are no simple solutions, Raj! We came to this country to fulfill our dreams and ambitions. Despite all odds, I think we have done well. We have to find our way and God will guide us in the right direction! Don't forget that ever, buddy!!"

Chandu was always optimistic that better times were ahead. That was true for Capricorns!!

Like mountain goats, they would reach the top after a hard and long climb!!

"I don't know how you do it, Chandu! But, thanks for talking to me! I am glad that you are there for me! I remember my mother's words when she let me come to USA so long as you were with me! Go back to bed!" Raj was ready to hang up.

"Now that I am already wide awake, I can't go back to bed, boy! I am getting up and making myself a strong cup of coffee before Kay gets up! Talk to you soon, bye!!"

Chandu thought about the concerns Raj had brought up during the phone call.

Maybe he should have suggested to Raj to seek some counseling. Maybe a psychologist or a psychiatrist. He decided that he would bring that up next time he talked to Raj.

"Who were you talking to, that early?" Kay asked Chandu when she came down.

"That was my buddy, Raj! He is really worried about his finances. His wife is not very helpful! She makes things worse for him. She is always blaming him for not trying harder. No wonder he is depressed! So, I gave him my ear and put in a few words. I feel bad for the guy! I thought I had it bad!!" Chandu sipped his coffee. "Well, we have a full day at the office, Kay! Hope I will be on time finishing my procedures at the hospital."

"Oh! You know! Elena is coming to see you today at the office. Don't forget!"

Chapter Sixty

Chandu got to his office on time. Procedures at the hospital went very smooth and he was quite happy that Marcy was his assistant. Kay was already preparing lunch in the small kitchen. Usually they would have soup or sandwich for a quick lunch before the patients would start coming. Sometimes a drug rep would show up around lunch time! They would also offer to bring in lunch once or twice a month. Chandu was quite popular with them since he was the speaker for the promotion of their products. Chandu was an excellent speaker and a teacher, and usually drew big audiences.

"Hi! Hon! What time is Elena coming to talk to me? You know?"

"She is coming around 4:30 this afternoon. I told her you should be done with your patients by then," Kay told Chandu after she handed him the bowl of soup.

Chandu liked the minestrone soup, but he would slip in a pinch of red chili pepper powder to make it spicy!!

"Hope we will get our medicare payment checks today, Kay! We have a lots of bills to pay this month! I have my malpractice insurance premium due also!"

"I have not gotten the mail yet. I guess we have a new mailman covering for Mark! This guy always comes in late. I hate that!!" Kay meant it!

Just as they finished their soup, the first patient walked in. Ronnie was always early for his appointment. He had to come all the way from Rochester, an hour's drive in normal weather conditions. If there was a snow storm, it would take him three hours!

"You know! Maybe you should find a gastroenterologist right near you! Why don't you?" Chandu would tease him. He had taken care of Ronnie when he was doing the residency training at the V.A. Hospital. As soon as Ronnie found out that Chandu was

was back and in private practice, he showed up at the office. Ronnie had a very severe intestinal condition called Crohn's disease and had undergone many, many surgeries. Now that he was under care of Chandu, his condition was very stable and he had not required any more surgeries. For this, he was immensely grateful and would go to great lengths to be treated by Chandu.

"You know Elena! She also worked at the hospital weight loss program!!"

"Of course I do! I remember her Hungarian goulash very well!! Do you still make that, Elena?" Chandu smiled.

"Yes! Dr. Chandu! I know both of you like it!! Maybe I can make you some when I come here to work!" Elena was almost sure she would be hired!

"What is your husband, Warner, doing now?" Chandu asked.

"Oh! He just took retirement! Now we have two grandkids and we want to spend time with them! That's why I told Kay that I can work three days part time, and that leaves us enough time to play with grandkids!"

"That sounds good, Elena! You know, you can work per diem and, of course, you will be covered by workman's comp if anything happens! You have to have your own health insurance. I hope you understand! You can help with the billing. Kay will do all the primary billing and you can do the secondary stuff, calling insurance companies, etc."

"I can handle that. I have my own Blue Cross & Blue Shield insurance which I will be able to keep." Elena was satisfied. At the hospital she had to work under a terrible supervisor! She was happy to get away from that environment.

"You want to work Monday, Wednesday & Fridays, then?" Chandu was flexible.

This was the third day in a row Raj had called Chandu early in the morning.

"I had to talk to you, buddy! As you know, I went to see Dr.Jaffri, the psychiatrist. He has got me on an antidepressant medication. I don't know if I can stay on it. I am experiencing side effects. I get nightmares and I feel anxious and irritable!! What do you think I should do? I can't live like this, boy!!" Raj was looking for answers.

"Hey! If you are having problem with the drug, you should call Jaffri and maybe he can change it to something else. I mean, there are so many drugs now! I am sure you will be able to tolerate one of them! But you need the medication, especially if he thinks so!! Don't give up, O.K.? Raj, you have to take care of yourself."

"Well, that's why I keep calling you!! Maybe I will stay on the drug for another two or three weeks and see what happens."

"That is the smart thing to do, Raj! As you know these drugs take at least a month or two before they work! Hang in there!!"

"Thank you for listening to me, Chandu! Sorry! I keep bothering you early in the morning. That's the only time I can call you when Malathi is still asleep!! I don't want her to know what is going on!"

"Hey! It's no bother! You can call me any time if you need me! Take care!"

Chandu was beginning to worry about his buddy. All he can do is to talk to him and encourage him to do the right thing.

Raj came to the office after finishing surgeries at the hospital. Kimmy was in the office. Chris, the office manager, was off sick that day.

"Hi! Raj! You are stuck with me, today! Chris is sick with the flu! Where do you want me to start?" Kimmy had a big smile on her face.

Raj came close to her, bent over and kissed her on her lips! Thank God there were no patients yet in the office!

"Kimmy! I am so glad you are here today! I had been feeling bad all morning! You are like a breath of fresh air!! Just don't leave me." Raj hugged her again.

"What makes you think I would leave you, Raj! Ever since I babysat at your place, I always wanted to be loved by you! I am glad I have that chance now!! I will make full use of this opportunity!! I know you are married and everything. But this is the next best thing for me!!" Kimmy kissed him passionately.

"Well, let's get to work, Kimmy!! I see someone walking in through the door! I don't want any one to suspect anything about us! O.K.?"

"My lips are sealed, Doc!!" Kimmy winked as she moved to the front desk.

The mail was already on his desk and Raj started sifting through the mail. There was a letter from a law firm asking to provide copies of medical records of a patient he had operated on two years ago. This one had died of complications after surgery because of underlying problems he had, heart and kidney problems.

The malpractice insurance carrier had advised him to let them know whenever a law firm requested medical records. So far, Raj had not been involved with any lawsuits. He had testified as an expert in some workman's compensation cases.

"One more thing to worry about," Raj thought and picked up the phone to call the insurance carrier for advice.

Chapter Sixty-Two

Brown Funeral Home was nestled in a busy residential area of suburban Orchard Place. The parking lot was getting filled up with expensive cars, and dark suited doctors and their wives were slowly entering the hallway of this big, old funeral home.

Chandu was standing by the ornate doorway greeting many friends and family members who knew Raj or had worked with him at the hospital.

There was a somber mood in the air, and in the background a tape player was echoing soothing chanting of some Hindu scriptures.

By the wall, surrounded by multiple colorful wreaths of flowers, was the open casket. Raj's body was dressed in his favorite striped blue suit and a bright red tie and shiny black shoes.

His eyes were shut, but one could almost discern a faint smile on his face. The funeral home had done a great job on embalming. His arms were folded across his chest and the long sleeved shirt had shiny cufflinks. His hair was dark, mixed with few strands of grey hair.

"He looks to be very much in peace with himself! Don't you think so, Chandu?" Dr. White asked as he fought back tears.

"He sure does, Doc! Now he has not a darn thing to worry about! He left that all for us!" Chandu answered as he was looking down the casket.

Prabhakar, Nabha and Gopal were also there greeting the mourners and talking to them.

"Why did this happen? He was such a great surgeon! We are really going to miss him." Dr.Barone was recalling how much he liked Raj.

"I know! He had always worried about coming to the race track! He didn't want to be away from the family."

The hospital administrator, Sister Eileen and other nuns that worked at the hospital, came to show their respect.

"So, you are Chandu! We have heard about you so much! You were his closest friend! Too bad, none of us expected anything like this. He was so young and such a skilled doctor! We surely are going to miss him!" Sister Eileen continued, "May God bless his soul and we pray for the family."

Malathi, Jitu and Reena were in one corner surrounded by some other family members from out of town. Malathi could hardly respond to anyone except to say with tears, "Thank you for coming. We will be O.K."

Chandu was watching the people as they came to the casket, stood and prayed.

He saw a beautiful curly haired blonde come to the casket who stood there silently for at least five minutes. She was sobbing as she gently touched Raj's hair and blew a kiss.
Chandu looked at her again and it dawned on him.

"This must be Brenda! Raj used to talk about her a lot! She was his surgical nurse!"

Chandu walked over to her as she was leaving the hall and laid his hands over her shoulder and said, "You must be Brenda! Aren't you? My buddy, Raj had lots of nice things to say about you! I guess he always liked you as his assistant in all his surgeries. My name is Chandu! Raj and I have known each other for a very long time! We went to the same medical school in India, Brenda. We came to this country together!" Chandu sighed as he fought back the tears.

"I know who you are, Chandu! Raj always thought very highly of you! I feel like I have known you for a long time! It is a real shame, what happened. We miss him!" Brenda wiped her tears.

Chapter Sixty-Three

There was a light drizzle early in the morning. Now the sky was clear and bright.

Sun had lit up the Elm Lawn Cemetery trees and buildings. Slowly the funeral caravan arrived through the gates. There were at least fifty or more cars, lots of nurses and other health care personnel that knew Raj, a number of doctors and friends of the family were among the attendees. After the Hindu priest said his prayers in front of the closed casket, he introduced Chandu.

"It is only appropriate that the family of Raj has requested Chandu, closest friend of Raj to deliver the final eulogy. Dr.Chandu, will you please do the honors?"

Chandu, who was seated in the front row of the auditorium got up quietly and walked over to the podium with a prepared note. He had worked on this for hours not knowing where to begin or how to end. He had not slept the whole night and dark circles were quite evident. He looked at the casket which was covered by a large wreath of flowers and looked up at the sky, closed his eyes for a brief second and faced the gathering.

He started reading the prepared eulogy in a slow and deliberate fashion. He had taken few passages from the holy scripture of Bhagavad-Gita, Bible of Hindu religion.

"Dear Friends and Family!

We are gathered here today, not to mourn the loss of our dearest friend and brother, Raj, but to celebrate his wonderful life.

Lord Krishna tells the sorrowing Arjuna in Chapter Eleven of Sankhyayoga or Yoga of knowledge, "Arjuna, you grieve over those who should not be grieved for, and yet speak like the learned. Wise men do not sorrow over the dead or the living." The Lord goes on to say, "Just as boyhood, youth and old age are attributed to the soul through this body, even so it attains another body. The wise man does not get deluded about this." The Lord says, "The soul is never born nor dies! Nor does it exist on coming into being. For, it is unborn, eternal, everlasting and primeval, even though the body is slain, the soul is not."

It was a cold and snowy refreshing afternoon in March of 1964, that the two of us arrived in this adopted country. Little did we know, what the future would bring. Here we were, in a far off place, some twelve thousand miles away from home land, with high hopes for a great education and training. I must say, we had the greatest of fun times through those learning years. Years of dedicated hard work & determination, we achieved the highest of our goals. We made our parents very proud.

Even as I read this, I can see you smile from heaven.

Raj, I have known you for over forty Years, thirty three of those here in Buffalo, our new home. We had fun times, times of exaltation and exuberance, extreme stressful situations in both of our lives, but we always managed to hold up our heads high and carried our expected roles. What else can I say about a friend of your caliber?

Remember the days, when our attending physicians knew we were on call, how we used to carry the load. Late night snacks on the sixth floor kitchen, the crazy card games, the late night TV shows, watching Johnny Carson, the nights at the race track, I could go on and on!

I was your best man at your wedding, and "Uncle Chandu" to your kids!! You were there for me and my family when I needed your shoulder.

If I can quote from the scriptures again, Lord Krishna says, "He who is free from malice towards all beings, who is friendly as well as compassionate, and is free from egoism, to whom pleasure and pain are alike and who is forgiving by nature, who is content and mentally united to me, who has subdued his body, mind and senses, and has a firm resolve, who has surrendered his mind and intellect to me, that devotee of mine is dear to me."

Raj, you were all that and more for sure. Now we all know why God loved you so much.

All those that are here today, and those that could not be with you but have you in their hearts, pray for your soul the eternal peace and tranquility that you so richly deserve.

I know how proud of your children you were. I can assure you that Anoop, Jitu, and Reena will carry on in your great tradition. Your dreams will be their goals. We all pray that your dear wife, Malathi, will gain the courage and determination to fulfill the unfinished task at hand with the help of all of us, friends and family members, and of course, the blessings of Lord Himself.

Well, my friend! I have to say goodbye for now, 'till we meet again at a place where there is no pain, no suffering, no illness, but a place full of laughter and eternal sunshine
May God bless your soul."

When Chandu finished, the whole crowd stood up and gave him a warm applause while tears were rolling down the cheeks of many.

The body was cremated as per the traditions, and the ashes were handed over to the priest. The next day, there was a special ceremony at Raj's home where the Hindu priest performed an elaborate divine prayer in front of a sacred fire pit. The oldest son, Anoop, had to be in charge of final rituals invoking God's blessings for the departed soul. Chandu was overcome with emotion as he watched Anoop follow the instructions from the priest.

As per the wishes of Raj, the ashes would be scattered over the Niagara River and also sent to India with the relatives to be scattered in the holy waters of the Ganges river in Varanasi.

Chapter Sixty-Four

"Prabhakar, I want you to be in charge as far as my financial affairs are concerned. I trust you more than anybody. Will you call Luca, the financial advisor and find out how the money situation is? Will you, Prabhakar? Malathi always had a special feeling for him.

"Of course, I will do that, Malathi. I will call Luca and make an appointment with him to discuss the financial matters. By the way did you hear from the insurance company about Raj's policy?" Prabhakar was curious. He wondered if the policy covered death by suicidal act.

"Actually, the agent called and he wanted a certified copy of the death certificate."

"That should be no problem, Malathi, I will take care of it."

"You know, Raj had bought a million dollar policy. I guess he knew that would take care of the kid's education and the home mortgage." Malathi continued,

"I don't want you tell this to any one, Prabhakar, I trust you!"

"I promise that I won't tell this to anybody, Malathi. Let me call Luca right now and make an appointment with him. You can come with me and we can talk about all of this! O.K.?"

"I really appreciate this, Prabhakar. Thank you for doing this. Raj always handled our finances and I just don't know what's what!" Malathi sighed.

"I know, the children are too young and you need help," Prabhakar agreed.

The next day Prabhakar picked up Malathi and drove to Luca's office in Amherst.

"Sorry about the loss, Malathi, I am really sorry. Raj was such a great doctor! He had so much going for him How are the kids handling?" Luca was very sincere.

"Thank you, Luca. I know Raj always thought very highly of you and your advice on financial matters. That's why we are here. I know you take care of Prabhakar and also Chandu, good friends of Raj. Where do we stand right now?"

Luca punched some keys on his desk top computer and brought up the brokerage account of Raj.

"Looking at the portfolio, the account has done very well. Once you get the death benefit from the insurance company, I want to set up a separate trust, with you as primary beneficiary and you can name the children as secondary. I think that would give you peace of mind. I think it is also good to pay off any credit card loans you have. You may have to open a separate bank account in your name. I will work with the attorney on setting up the trust. How does that sound to you, Prabhakar?" Luca turned to him.

"You are the expert, Luca! I only deliver babies and do surgery! You take care of our money!" Prabhakar laughed.

"You are going to be fine, Malathi! Your kids are going to do well. I know Jitu is going to medical school. He will follow in his father's footsteps, I am sure!"

"Well, by God's blessing I hope so too, Luca! Is there anything else I need to do?"

"No, Malathi. I will take care of the paper work and if I need you, I can call you or call Prabhakar and he can contact you. O.K.?"

"That is fine, Luca. I want to thank you again for all that you have done and I am sure Raj is looking down from heaven appreciating your help!"

Prabhakar got up and Malathi followed him after they said goodbye to Luca. Malathi felt a strange sensation of satisfaction and a faint smile flashed.

Chapter Sixty-Five

"Kay! I have been thinking about Raj! You know it has already been a month since he is gone, I always wondered why I didn't get a call from him that fateful morning. He had called me four or five days in a row around the same time early morning! Maybe if he had called, maybe, I would have been able to talk to him I don't really know if I could have prevented what happened! But I wonder!"

"Honey! I know you tried your best talking to him whenever you had a chance. You told me that he was really depressed about a lot of things. Always worried about his finances and his kids education. I don't think we can ever guess what pushed him over the edge. We may never know, do you think?" Kay knew how much Chandu encouraged Raj about keeping faith and thinking positive.

"I think of his mother, Kay! When we left India, she was so happy that we were going to USA together and I would be there to watch him as a brother! I feel like I failed somehow! That bothers me the most ." Chandu sighed.

"Dear, you did your best. Unfortunately, Malathi was not very supportive! I think she pushed him to the limits. He was working so hard. Two or three jobs! He didn't have to, you know. I guess she was spoiled by her close friends and their demands."

"That is true. After his second marriage, how many times did we get invited to his home? She kind of kept him away from his very close buddies. Even Nabha and Gopal expressed the same feelings when we got together at the funeral home."

"She was very close to her friends from Bombay! I don't blame her! I guess they spoke the same language and had similar interests! She was very comfortable in their circle!"

"You are right, Kay! I know you women have instincts, you can pick up stuff that we men can't!"

"Well, are we ready to have soup? I know we have a lot of patients today! Just before we go on vacation to Ohio!" Chandu started looking through some of the lab reports.

"The usual mushroom soup and crackers, Dear! I don't know what we will have for dinner. Kids do their own thing! We have to think for us! Maybe something on the grill!" Kay got busy in the little kitchen preparing soup.

The telephone rang and Kay grabbed the phone.

"Hi! Is this Dr.Chandu's office?" The voice on the line was somewhat shaky.

"Yes! Who is calling, please?" Kay could not recognize the person at the other end.

"This is personal. I need to talk to the doctor! This is very important! I must talk to him, please!" the caller pleaded. Kay could appreciate the urgency and also the seriousness in the caller's voice.

"Just a minute, please! I will see if he is free." She put the caller on hold and came to Chandu.

"Honey! There is a lady on the phone. She really wants to talk to you. She is very serious and says this is very important! Shall I put her on?"

"O.K.! I am not sure what this is about or who she is. Put her on!" Chandu had no clue.

" Hi! This is Dr.Chandu! How can I help you?"

"Dr. Chandu, my name is Kimmy! I have something very important to talk to you about! It involves your dear friend, Raj! I have to see you in person! I can't talk on the phone. After work can you call me at this number? 555-7794, please!"

Chandu wrote down the number and told her that he would call after work.

"Let's get going, Kay! I will finish the paper work tomorrow. I am still thinking about this call from Kimmy! For some reason, I think I know this girl! I have this feeling that Raj had mentioned her name some time! I wish I could remember." Chandu was thinking hard.

"You will soon find out who this is, Honey! You are supposed to call her after we get home!" Kay was curious as well.

"Let's stop by Wegman's and pick up a couple of rib eye steaks! That sounds good to me! I can throw them on the grill, maybe with some fresh corn on the cob! What do you say?"

"That will be fine with me as long as I can have my mashed potatoes!!" Kay replied. "You can have your meat and potatoes!! Maybe after dinner, I can call that girl."

They stopped at the grocery store on Transit Road near their home and picked up the meat and a couple of ears of corn. Chandu realized that they were out of wine and stopped at the Premier Liquor place and grabbed a couple of bottles of Sterling Merlot and a bottle of Great Western Champagne which they always enjoyed with dinner.

After dinner, Chandu called the telephone number Kimmy had given him.

"Hi! This is Dr. Chandu, Kimmy! Tell me how to get to your place and I can meet you."

"I live at Amherst Towers apartment complex near Harlem road, Dr.Chandu. You know where that is? My apartment number is twelve. I live by myself. You can ring the bell and I will let you in!"

"I am sure I can find the place, Kimmy! I will see you in about twenty minutes."

Chandu had no problem finding the place. On the way over, he remembered what Kay told him! "Be very careful, Honey! We don't know what this girl is up to! I hope she is not some kind of a nut case! Just watch yourself! I love you!"

Chandu rang the bell after he got on the elevator and reached the third floor. The door opened and at the door was a beautiful young lady dressed in jeans and a tight red sweater showing off nice curvaceous figure. She had bright blue eyes.

"I am so glad you came, Dr.Chandu! I feel like I have known you for years!!

I used to baby-sit your buddy's kids when I was in high school. Then I worked at his office during summer time when I was home from college! I am sure your friend, Raj, must have mentioned my name, talked about me! Right?"
Now it hit Chandu! No wonder! The name rang a bell!!

"Of course, Kimmy! Now I know who you are! He always had a very soft heart for you. You were very special to him!"

"Well! Not just special, Chandu! More than that. I was very much in love with him ever since I laid my eyes on him! The feeling was mutual!" Kimmy walked over to the little b.ar and pulled a bottle of Johnny Walker Black Label scotch! That was Raj's favorite brand of scotch! On the wall near the hall way there was a nice picture of Raj, in casual dress, holding a book. He looked very happy in that picture. Kimmy mixed a couple of glasses of scotch and club soda, dropped in a few chunks of ice, and handed it to Chandu.

"Here is to your friend, my dear Raj! He wanted to make sure I met with you some day! We used to get together at least once or twice a week here and enjoy each other's company! After a hard day's work and a tough day at home, he really enjoyed being with me and relaxing, having a couple of glasses of scotch! Talking about his life and talking about how the two of you came to this country!"

Chandu touched her glass with his and took a sip of the smooth scotch.

"I knew he would come to medical meetings in the area and used to take off early. I knew it wasn't always emergency calls! So, this is where he would come and relax! One thing I must say about my buddy! He was very smooth!!"
Chandu continued, "Tell me what was it that you really wanted to see me about?"

"You know that Raj had a very tough personal life at home, I mean with his wife. I am sure you know he had been seeing a psychiatrist and was put on medications."

"I am aware of that, Kimmy! I also know he was having problems with some side effects."

"Chandu! I am going to tell you something that no body knows!" Kimmy sat close to Chandu.

Chandu's heart started pounding! "What is it Kimmy? You can tell me."

"Remember! A few months ago he was in the hospital?"

"Of course I do! I went to see him at the hospital."

"Remember! He said that he was weak from the flu and fell down the basement stairs?" "Yeah! He hit his head and they kept him in for observation for concussion!"

"That was just a story he made up, Chandu! What happened was," Kimmy started sobbing.

Chandu leaned over and held her hand. "Come on! You can tell me, Kimmy!"

"It was actually a trial run for suicide! I guess he attempted to commit suicide but he did not have the right technique! He fell down on the floor hitting his head. His wife, Malathi, didn't know about this. He talked about this when he was here! Only after a couple of drinks!!"

"I guess he had perfected this after his failed attempt! Being a surgeon, he knew how to tie knots! Oh! My God!! What a way to end the life?" Chandu also had tears in his eyes.

"But, but! Chandu! He also told me how many times he really thought about ending his life, but after he would talk to you, he would be O.K. for a few days. She continued, you really kept him going. He felt bad that he couldn't spend more time with you! Now that I have got it off my chest, I feel better, Chandu! I am so glad that you came to visit me. I feel like your friend, Raj, is at peace with himself!!"

"His kids are all doing well, Kimmy! That's what I always worried about. I am glad he had a great friend in you! You were there for him to lean on! You should feel very happy to have made his life a little better. I am grateful to you for being there for him. I know we can never bring him back! But let's us think of his rich life and all those he helped heal along the way! Take care of yourself." Chandu held her close and gave her a warm hug.

About the Author

Dr.Charles Narasi is a board certified gastroenterologist and a senior fellow of American College Of Gastroenterology. He was in private practice with offices in Tonawanda, N.Y. and was an active staff member of Kenmore Mercy Hospital in Kenmore, N.Y. He was the president of the medical staff 1995-1996. He was also the president of G.I. & Liver Society of Western N.Y. in 2004. After nearly forty years of serving the community of greater Buffalo, he is now retired and lives in Stockbridge,Georgia with his wife, Karen. He enjoys teaching, traveling, gardening, photography and especially cooking. This novel depicts some of his interesting travel experiences and facts about aspects of adjustment when he came to this country, his new home.